YOU CAN TRUST ME

KIERSTEN MODGLIN

KIERSTEN
MODGLIN
Love Lies Alibis

Cover Design by Kiersten Modglin
Copy Editing by Three Owls Editing
Proofreading by My Brother's Editor
Formatting by Kiersten Modglin
Copyright © 2023 by Kiersten Modglin.
All rights reserved.

First Print and Electronic Edition: 2023
kierstenmodglinauthor.com

To my family—for the cruise in 2019 that I was sure would lead to disaster but actually only resulted in a sunburn and nightmares.

To my readers, the KMod Squad—for requesting a cruise thriller so those nightmares didn't go to waste.

"For all evils there are two remedies - time and silence."

ALEXANDRE DUMAS, *THE COUNT OF MONTE CRISTO*

PART 1

CHAPTER ONE

BLAKE

It's always the husband.

That's what they say anyway, isn't it? I've probably said it once or twice myself while watching the news or reading a book. It's clichéd, but the reality is it's almost always true.

Almost always.

But not now.

Not this time.

You've already cast your judgment. I won't waste my time trying to change your mind, but, for the record, you couldn't be more wrong about me.

I didn't do this.

I love her.

You can trust me.

CHAPTER TWO

MAE

BEFORE

This place should feel like paradise, but for me, it will always be a reminder of heartbreak.

Even with years of better memories to replace that first visit—sun-soaked summers with my favorite people—I can't let go of the past. Can't forget what happened. What this beach bore witness to.

I died here, in a way. There's the me before and the me after, and the two will never be the same.

Today, the sun warms my skin, and the salty breeze whips through my hair as sand collects in my sandals. It's beautiful here. I can say that objectively. I get the appeal. Truly I do, but I can't look at the sand or the ocean, hear the seagulls cawing overhead, or smell the fishy smell of the water without thinking of him.

Blake's fingers lace with mine as the restaurant comes into view. "Is she here yet?"

I lift my phone with my opposite hand, staring at the screen. One of our wedding photos stares back at me, taking my breath away as much now as they did the day we received them. We look so happy...

It's been almost a year, and somehow I'm still not quite used to the weight of the ring on my finger.

"I don't think so. She hasn't texted. I'll let her know where they seat us when they do."

"Sounds good. Hopefully they have space on the patio. It's so nice out." He releases my hand to let me up the wooden set of stairs to the boardwalk first.

As if to further prove his point, the wind picks up again, blowing the warm air around us. It's the perfect temperature, before the heat of the summer completely arrives, but still warm enough to enjoy.

Inside the small restaurant, a dark-haired host greets us.

I glance at the nametag on their shirt, which reads **Hayden (They/them)**.

"Hey guys, how many?"

"Four," Blake says, holding up four fingers. "We're waiting on two others."

"Cool. Inside or patio?"

"Patio would be awesome."

Hayden grabs a stack of menus. "You got it. Follow me." They lead the way around through the small space and back out onto the patio, where two tables are occupied by an older couple and a woman around our age with a little boy. He's scribbling away at a coloring page as we follow Hayden toward a table near the end of the space. The string lights above our heads sway in the wind as we take our seats.

"Destiny will be your waitress today. Can I get you started with some drinks, or would you like her to come over once the rest of your party has arrived?"

Blake checks with me, though I know he's starving. "We can go ahead and order drinks if you want. They should be here any minute."

He gestures for me to go first, so I order a ginger ale, hoping it will ease the nausea I still feel over our flight. Then he orders a beer. I do my best to withhold a bitter glance his way. I'd been okay with the drinks on the plane so early because I know he's a nervous flier, but we're on land now.

Hayden takes our menus, promising to be right back, and I watch as a bird hops around on a table next to us, picking french fries off a plate yet to be cleaned.

"So, what do we know about this one?" Blake asks, keeping his voice low. He's not wrong to sound so pessimistic, but for Florence's sake, I'm trying not to be.

"Um, not much. His name is Patton. He's two years older than her and he runs some sort of tech startup. He jogs every morning and likes breakfast foods. I think that's all she's mentioned."

"A tech startup, hmm? Well, that's...impressive."

"Yeah, I think so." He's quiet for a moment as I send Florence a text to let her know where we're seated. "At least he has a job." I place the phone down on the table. "She seems to really like this one. I'm glad he could come

6

with us on this trip. For her sake. I know she always hates feeling like the third wheel."

He runs a hand through his dark hair as Hayden reappears with our drinks. "I told Destiny you're waiting for two others, so she'll be over as soon as they get here. Let us know if you need anything in the meantime."

"Thanks." I tear the paper from my straw and tuck it under the metal napkin holder so it doesn't blow away.

"Oh. There she is." I turn in my seat at Blake's words just as Florence appears on the stairs.

She's alone. Her jet-black hair has been pulled back in a sleek ponytail, the ends of which brush her deeply tanned skin. I lift a hand, waving at her until I catch her eye and she waves back, smiling.

Within minutes, Hayden leads her to our table. She kisses my cheek briefly before easing into the empty seat next to me. "So good to see you guys. Sorry I'm late."

"Where's Patton?" I ask.

"Oh." She waves a hand in the air nonchalantly, though she's unable to hide the disappointment in her tone. "He got stuck on a work call but didn't want to hold us up. He should be here later, but we don't have to wait on him." She looks over my head. "Have you ordered yet? I'm starving."

"No, we were waiting. Are you sure he wants us to go ahead and order? Maybe we should just start with drinks and an appetizer or something," I offer.

She pulls her phone from the royal-blue clutch resting on the table and taps the screen. "No, it's fine. He could be a while."

"Okay, I'll go let Hayden know there's been a change of plans," Blake says, standing up.

Once he's gone, I turn to Florence once again. "How are things? Did you guys get in okay?"

"Yep," she says. "The flight was fine and our room is nice." She pats the table expectantly. "How about you guys? Everything okay? How are you feeling?"

She knows the truth without me having to say it, but I do anyway. "I'm hanging in there. Every year gets a bit easier." I pause. "It helps, having you guys here with me this year with...everything." My voice catches in my throat. I can't bring myself to finish the sentence.

She draws one side of her mouth in with a sympathetic nod. "Of course. We wouldn't be anywhere else. We'll keep the tradition alive even if... No matter what happens." She sucks in a long breath, realizing she's said too much, almost led herself down a path she didn't mean to go. Blake saves us both by returning to the table and sliding into his chair.

"The waitress is on her way."

Beside me, Florence is beaming suddenly, and Blake appears unamused. He gives her a devilishly suspicious look. "What? Did you tell her?"

She shakes her head. "No, but *can* we already? I'm dying here."

Probably not the best choice of words, but I'd be a terrible person to point that out, so I don't. Besides, my curiosity is piqued. "Tell me what? What's going on?"

"There you are." A voice behind us startles me, and I

look over my shoulder, expecting to recognize the man standing there. I don't. He's average height, late twenties or early thirties, with thick brown hair, dark skin, and a chiseled jaw. He's attractive in an in-your-face sort of way, with muscles for days and a prize-winning smile. My eyes jerk up to meet his, still trying to understand who he is and why he knows me, when Florence shoots up from her chair.

"There *you* are!" she shrieks, swatting his chest as he wraps an arm around her waist. She leans back as they both grin at us like a pair of Instagram models. They look so good together it's painful. "You got here faster than I expected. Guys, this is Patton. Patton, this is my best friend in the *whole* world, Mae, and her husband, Blake."

We each extend a hand and he shakes them one at a time. "Nice to meet you both. Sorry I'm late. I got stuck on a call with my office that ran over. I hope it won't ruin your first impression of me."

"No. No problem," Blake says.

"It's totally fine," I say at the same time. "We get it."

He kisses the side of her head near her temple and pulls away as the waitress approaches.

"You're beside Blake," Florence tells Patton, gesturing toward the empty seat. We return to the table as the waitress, whose name tag reads **Destiny (She/her)**, reaches us.

She takes their drink orders while the two new arrivals read over their menus, and when she returns moments later, we place our orders and pass the menus back to her.

Once we're alone again, I eye my husband. "So, what are you supposed to be telling me?"

His gaze falls to Florence, and they seem to have a silent conversation I'm not yet privy to.

"Okay. You guys are freaking me out. What's going on?" I demand, trying to keep my tone light, though I feel quite the opposite.

Florence rests her hands flat on the table, turning her head to look at me slowly. She inhales. "We have a sort of...surprise for you."

"A surprise?"

"Yes. Hopefully it's a good one. We're, uh, we're going on a cruise!" She winces as she says it, though her face is lit up like she's been bursting to tell me. And I guess she has been.

It takes me a few seconds to process what she's said. "A cruise? What? *When?*"

This is my only week of vacation time, and I can't afford to take any more time off. Blake knows this, so why does he look so happy?

"Tomorrow." She beams at me, lips pinched together, all prim and proper. "For five days."

Time stops for half a second. Tomorrow is impossible. This has to be a joke. "*Tomorrow,* tomorrow? How? Where? I didn't bring my passport. We're already checked into the hotel for the week. We're supposed to be here." I don't mean to sound as angry as I do, but I hate last-minute changes in plans. Especially when I'm the only one who seems to not have been made aware of them.

"I packed your passport," Blake speaks up. "And I only made the hotel reservation for the night."

"What? Why?"

"We wanted to surprise you," Florence says, her voice softer than it was when she last spoke. My reaction has thrown her off. "I, er, well, *we* thought... I knew you wanted to be here for the anniversary, but since it's the first year that your parents couldn't come with you... I just thought it might be nice to change it up a bit. Do something new."

I don't know what to say, but it's obvious I need to say something. Florence's confidence is waning by the minute, her smile fading like a time-lapse video. I can't help feeling guilty.

"We thought you'd like it," Blake says gently. "Was it a bad idea?"

"No." I force myself to say it with a grin plastered on my face. "No, of course not. It's really sweet. I just... I'm processing. So"—I let out a sigh—"we're going on a cruise? And we leave tomorrow?"

"Yes. We're going to Costa Maya and Cozumel." Florence squeaks with excitement. "It's going to be so much fun."

"Wow. So, it's real... It's, like, real then? How long've you been planning this?"

The three of them exchange glances.

"Well..." Blake shifts his gaze back to me. "Florence asked me what I thought right after we found out your parents weren't going to be able to make it this year. We wanted to do something to make the trip extra special for you but couldn't decide what. We booked the cruise two weeks ago. It was all very last minute."

"Patton's company does some IT work for the cruise line, so he got us a stellar deal, which I know you'll appreciate," Florence teases, nudging me gently.

"I do love a good deal... How did you manage to keep it a secret?" I ask.

Blake chuckles. "Well, it wasn't easy. I almost slipped up more than once. But I put it on my credit card so you wouldn't notice the charges. That was the biggest thing."

"And you planned...everything?"

"Well, Florence planned most of it. She just told me what to do."

That sounds more believable. My husband is chronically allergic to planning, so this feels impossible.

"Are you mad?" Florence asks, sounding hurt. "We thought you'd be excited. I just knew this year, without your parents here, it might be harder than usual. I wanted to help...take your mind off of things, I guess."

Taking my mind off of things seems rather counterproductive since the whole reason we come here every year is to think about what happened here, to remember what we lost. *Who* we lost.

I don't say that.

Can't.

"I'm not mad. Honestly, I'm just shocked, is all. I've

never really thought about going on a cruise." *For good reason*, though I don't say that part out loud. My brother was killed in a boating accident. Are they trying to be insensitive, or am I just being *overly* sensitive? This week always brings out the worst in me.

"We know that too. It'll be the first time for all of us. That's why we're doing this together." She loops her arm through mine. "It's going to be fun. Trust me. Have I ever steered you wrong?"

I eye her. We both know the answer to that question. Her judgment has, more than once, landed us stranded without a ride after a night of drinking or waking up in a house we didn't recognize. But those days are long gone. The wild college days of Florence and Mae are just distant memories.

She grins, and I finally give in, leaning a head onto her shoulder. "Okay, fine." I wink at Blake. "But just know I fully expect surprises like this for every holiday now."

His shoulders drop with relief, and he gives me a playful look. "Yeah, we've set ourselves up for some major letdowns in the future, haven't we?"

"You could never let me down." I pull away, reaching for his hand across the table. "But if this is our last night on the shore, we're going to need to do all the annual things tonight. Starting with an amazing dinner." I point across the restaurant as I spot Destiny making her way toward us with a tray in her hands.

"Sounds like a plan. Here's to an amazing vacation." Blake lifts his glass toward me.

"To a week we'll never forget," Florence chimes in, lifting her own glass.

Patton and I join in, tapping all four glasses in a circle in the air above the table, then I take a sip.

To a week we'll never forget.

CHAPTER THREE

BLAKE

"Will you unzip me?"

Mae turns around, holding her hair up with one hand as she waits for me to unzip the shirt she's wearing. I yawn, moving toward her. It's later than I planned to be out, really. The night is over. Checking my watch, I see it's ten minutes until it will technically be morning, and I'm so exhausted I feel ready to collapse on the bed without changing or brushing my teeth. If I closed my eyes for just ten minutes, I'd be out.

As I unzip her, I lean forward and press my lips to the space where her neck meets her shoulder, breathing in the salty scent of her skin.

She turns to face me, patting my cheek as she stares at me with a quiet sort of wonder. "You okay?"

"Just tired," I promise. I've also had a little bit too much to drink, but I suspect she knows that.

"Well, I guess we have an early morning, don't we? It probably wasn't the best idea to stay out so late."

"We'll survive it," I say, unbuttoning my shirt. "Besides, we don't have to board the ship until three tomorrow, so we can sleep in a bit."

"Yes, but Florence said we can board starting at eleven. I'd rather get on early if we can." She steps out of her pants, tossing her dirty clothes down and searching through her suitcase for a pair of pajamas. Once she has them on, she sits down on the edge of the bed.

I'm slipping into my own pajamas when I catch her eye in the mirror.

She smiles, but it's sad. Distant. I turn around at once.

"What is it?"

"I just can't believe you did all this for me." She says it with a long breath, like she's been holding it in all night.

"What do you mean?"

"The cruise. I know you said Florence did most of the work, but you've had so much on your plate lately at the office. I know this couldn't have been easy."

I sit down next to her, and she scoots a bit to give me space. "Honey, it doesn't matter. We just wanted to do something nice for you. I know this week is important to you. Remembering Danny matters to me, too. And to Florence. I know we didn't know him, but he would've been my brother-in-law. This week means something. And not having your parents here for the first time makes it all that much harder. I know you were imagining this differently and I couldn't get your parents here, but I wanted this year to be special in a new way." I wrap an arm around her shoulders, kissing her temple. "A new tradition, maybe."

She turns her head to kiss me. It's warm at first. Tempting. Her mouth opens, tongue searching. But just as quickly as it starts, she stops. She gives one last firm kiss that signals this will go no further tonight and then stands.

I'm still in a bit of a stupor when I hear her say, "Speaking of my parents, what did they say about all of this? Were they okay with us doing something different? I know they aren't here, but...you know what I mean. It was important to them. Staying here. On this shore. In this hotel. Where everything happened... It's always meant something to them, you know?"

I hesitate. I guess I hadn't thought of that. Maybe I didn't want to. "Right. Um, I haven't told them yet."

She waits for me to explain, her face frozen with an emotion I can't read.

"I just didn't want them to let something slip and ruin the surprise," I offer.

"No, I understand. It makes sense. It's just..."

"What?" I stand, moving toward her cautiously. I know this week is filled with a nuance I can't completely grasp, with painful memories and a sort of quiet dread that fills my wife and her parents in the days leading up to it and the months that follow. Losing someone like they lost Danny, when he was so young, it changes you in a way I'm fortunate not to relate to.

Some days, though, I wish I could. Selfish and stupid as it may be. Some days I wish I could understand.

Maybe it would help bridge the gap I can never seem to close between us.

It's as if my wife exists just beyond a glass wall. As if we can both press our hands to it, but we can never quite touch.

"I should call and tell them. They should know. I won't be able to talk to them all week..." She presses a finger to her lips, thinking. I don't know what I expected, honestly, but it wasn't this. When Florence pitched the idea, it seemed perfect. Now though, I can't help feeling we've made a mistake.

"We'll have Wi-Fi on the ship, so you should be able to text, maybe even make calls, though I read mixed reviews about how strong the signal is. The call quality might be terrible. Either way, I paid for the international calls plan this month, so you'll be able to check in when we're on land."

"Still, I should call and let them know."

"Of course. Don't you think you should wait to call them in the morning? There will be plenty of time. It's late tonight." I say this gently, simply as a suggestion.

She checks the clock on the nightstand. "It'll only be ten their time. Dad might still be awake."

I sigh, more from exhaustion than frustration. "Maybe. Hopefully. Give him a call if you think so." I rub her arm, then make my way into the bathroom to brush my teeth while she places the call.

Within seconds, I hear her voice.

"It's me. Did I wake you?" She pauses, listening to his response. "No, everything's fine. How's Momma?"

I turn on the water, drowning out the next few words. When I turn it off, she's talking again.

"I know. I wish you guys were here, too. Next year." Her voice is soft. We all know that even if her mom is well enough to come next year, her time is running out. She's beaten the odds for far too long. I cough to rid myself of the tickle in my throat.

"Um, I was just calling because..." She clears her throat, and I realize she's been crying. "We're going on a cruise this week. Florence and Blake surprised me with it. They thought since you guys couldn't be here, it would be a nice distraction for me."

I step closer toward the door, wanting desperately to hear her next words. How her parents react will set the tone for the trip. My in-laws are not unreasonable people, but once you lose a child, it makes you hold on to the one you have left a little tighter.

"No, I know. But it'll be okay. We'll all be together." She sniffles as I rest my toothbrush on the counter. Even my brushing makes it hard to hear her. "Well, I can't cancel it, Dad. It was a nice gesture. I promise I'll be okay." She sighs, and I start brushing again. "It's a big boat. A ship. Not like..." She can't bring herself to say the words, but they hang there anyway, and suddenly, I realize our mistake. This boat isn't like the boat Danny died on, but it's still a boat. It's the same ocean.

The same week.

I drop my head.

How could I have been so blind as to what this must drag up for them? It's my first year here with her, but she's told me enough about it over the years. I should've known better. Florence should've known better.

"I'll be fine. I know it's late. I just wanted to tell you. I'll check in when I can," she says in what seems like a single breath. Like she just has to get it out. "Kiss Momma for me. I love you."

When she appears in the doorway, fresh tears swim in her eyes, and I place my toothbrush down, wrapping her in my arms. "I didn't think..." I whisper. It's all I can bring myself to say.

"It's okay."

"We don't have to go. We can stay here. I'll figure it all out."

"No. I don't want that. It was a sweet gesture. I understand why you did it, and maybe you're right. Maybe I need this. Besides, this isn't like Danny."

It's not, but it is. And we both know it.

"He wasn't happy," she adds.

I nod. "I'm sorry."

"But he trusts you to keep me safe."

"I will," I swear to her. "You know I will."

"I know."

"Was he mad?"

"Not mad, just...not happy," she repeats. "I think he feels like we're betraying the tradition a little bit. Forgetting why we do this."

"Is that how you feel?"

She looks down, not answering. "He said we shouldn't go. He made it clear he doesn't want us to, but it's not his decision." She doesn't mean it in a malicious way. She's saying it more to herself, convincing herself it's the truth.

"Everything's going to be fine. He'll see. We aren't forgetting Danny. We're honoring his life. I have to believe he'd want you to be happy. To live."

She rests her head on my chest. "I know you're right. It's just...hard, I guess. I don't want to talk about it anymore, okay? I'm tired. Let's just go to bed."

And so we do.

CHAPTER FOUR

MAE

We're having breakfast in our room the next morning, slowly repacking our things as I wait for Florence to text to let us know they've woken up.

"Anything yet?" Blake asks, spying me checking my phone again.

"Nope."

"They both had a lot more to drink than I did. They'll probably sleep until fifteen minutes before we board," he says with a laugh.

"As long as they make it to the ship. What do you think of Patton, by the way? We never got to talk about him when we got back last night."

He stops in his tracks, hands loaded up with the travel soaps and mouthwash provided by the hotel. "He seems nice, I guess. Not really her type."

"What's that mean?"

"Well, he's..." He pauses, searching for the right word. "Kind of nerdy, I guess, isn't he?"

"Nerdy? Why do you say that?"

"He's in IT. And, well, I mean, talking to him... He seemed really put together. Like, 'smart' is a better word for it."

I laugh, caught off guard by his bluntness. "You're saying her type isn't smart guys?"

He eyes me, a glint of playfulness in his gaze. "You met her last boyfriend, didn't you?"

"What was wrong with Ted?" I cross my arms.

"Well, other than the fact that he was chronically unemployed and still said things like 'righteous' and 'right on, man'?" He draws his words out, sounding so much like Ted I have to laugh. "He once asked me if the name Blake was *short* for anything and, if you remember, he lost us a trivia game at Hank's because he said the capital of California was, *and I quote*, 'C.'"

My giggles grow louder. "Okay, okay. Fair enough. He wasn't exactly a scholar, but not all of her boyfriends have been that bad. Besides, she's entitled to date whoever she wants. Lars left her for her cousin a month before their wedding."

"Oh, I was there. You don't have to remind me," he says, dropping the items from his hands into his suitcase. "And anyway, I'm saying Patton seems cool. He could be good for her."

"Yeah, I think so. I like him, too."

"Yeah, we could all tell," he says with a mischievous look.

"What does that mean?"

He chuckles. "If I was an insecure man, I might've

been offended by how often you checked out his muscles."

"I did not!" I shriek, my face burning hot in an instant.

"Mm-hmm." He flexes dramatically. "These guns aren't enough for you, hmm?"

I swat at him in the air. "Oh, shut up. You know you have nothing to worry about."

"Nope, I guess I'll be spending the cruise in the gym. When we leave, I'll be able to deadlift you." He launches forward, lifting me into his arms. I laugh loudly as we fall forward onto the bed. He catches us, so the impact is lessened. I kiss his nose, brushing the dark hair from his eyes.

"You're ridiculous, you know that?"

"You love me."

"I do," I confirm, pressing my lips to his. At once, his muscles relax, his hand sliding down to grasp my side. His kiss is fierce, demanding. I didn't miss the way he pressed himself against me last night as we were falling asleep—an open invitation despite how exhausted we both were. I wasn't receptive then, but now... I feel my skin heating as his fingers explore my body, sliding under my shirt.

"I love you, too," he whispers, pulling back only slightly. "More than anything."

"More than everything," I vow, raising my hands so he can tug my shirt over my head.

Four hours later, the sun beats down on us through the windows of the gangway as we wait in line to board the ship. The line moves slowly, buzzing with excitement as we draw nearer to the entrance.

"Almost there," Florence squeals quietly, squeezing my arm from behind. I smile at her over my shoulder, careful not to trip on uneven footing. Through the cracks where the flooring meets, I see the ground several feet below. Concrete. Crew members milling about, loading our luggage through a different entrance.

My stomach churns with nerves I hadn't expected as we get closer to the ship's entrance. I never considered myself to be afraid of water, as much time as I spend at the beach, but a ship is a different story.

I know they wouldn't judge me if I admitted this, but I can't. I have to be brave, both for them and for myself.

"Once we're inside, we can go to the bar and get a drink or head to the casino. They usually have live music from what I read," Patton says. "It'll be a few hours before we can get to our rooms."

"A drink sounds nice," Blake says, tossing a look back over his shoulder. When he locks eyes with me, he tenses. "Maybe." It's slight, but I notice it.

It's still pretty early, and I want to remind him of that, but I know I can't without seeming like I'm nagging. It's a vacation, and I'm supposed to be relaxed. I just wish my body would get the hint.

It would be easier if we weren't being herded by the thousands like cattle onto this ship.

God, sometimes I don't know how anyone puts up

with me. My negativity, even internally, is so far past annoying that I can't understand how they still want to spend time with me.

No wonder he drinks so much.

When we reach the entrance to the ship, we step inside past the smiling crew members who welcome us and direct us to follow the crowd through the next set of doors, which lead to the ship's atrium. From there, they tell us we can go anywhere we'd like except our rooms.

In the atrium, I stop, looking up at the sun shining through the glass above us. Without realizing I'm doing it, I find myself spinning in a circle, wanting to take in every angle of the rainbow haze that fills the space.

It's beautiful and awe-inspiring, and for the first time since we left the hotel, I don't feel tense. It actually seems like this could be as magical as Blake and Florence have sold it to be.

An older man bumps into me, breaking the haze I'm in as he shoves past. His wife huffs on her way by without making eye contact. Blake pulls me closer to him, pinning them with an angry stare as Florence and Patton form an unintentional circle with us.

"You okay?" Blake asks.

"I'm fine." My cheeks heat with embarrassment. All around us, people are entering the ship and scattering, heading in every direction with a sort of intentionality, as if they know exactly where they're going. Maybe they do. I, on the other hand, feel utterly lost. Now that I'm not distracted by the view, the space is oddly disorienting. It's easy to forget we're on a ship at all rather than inside a hotel. I hear the sounds of people cheering in the distance, though I can't tell which direction it's coming from.

"Looks like the casino's that way," Patton says, staring at the map on his phone—pinning, zooming, and scrolling with two fingers to get a better look. "Or if you guys would rather just get something to drink, we can head up to the bar on the top deck. Elevators are that way, but reviews say they're usually slow, so we may want to take the stairs, which are just over there."

"Whatever you guys want," Florence says with a shrug. "I just want to find somewhere to sit down. My legs are killing me. I forgot how hard it is to walk in the sand."

"Casino sounds good to me. We can get a drink there," Blake says, nudging me gently. "That okay?"

"My man!" Patton says with a throaty laugh. "Let's go."

He turns and leads the way. Before it's in sight, the stale scent of cigarette smoke hits my nose. I inhale through my mouth, feeling ill. "People can smoke in here?"

Florence fans the odor from her own nose with a disgusted look on her face. "How is that still legal?"

"Casinos," Patton says as if it's enough of an explanation. "Does it bother you? We can go somewhere else."

Florence looks at me and I shake my head. "No, you guys go. I'm just going to sit over here for a while and check out the views." I jut a thumb at the window behind me.

"I'll stay with you," Blake says, and suddenly everyone's stopped, appearing ready to abandon the previous plan.

Thankfully, in the form of my saving grace, Florence steps toward me. "You boys go play. We'll get drinks, rest our feet, and breathe the fresh air." She links her arms with mine.

"Are you sure?" Blake asks, hesitating.

"Yeah, it's fine," I assure him. "You guys go have fun. I'll hang with Flo."

He stares at me for a few seconds longer, perhaps searching for a sign that I'll be angry about this later, but I just give him a big smile and turn to walk away with her.

"I need refreshments," she teases, squeezing me closer to her. "What do you say we find the bar?"

"Can we just sit down for a minute?" I ask, pointing to the large window ahead of us with a cloth bench seat in front of it. "I'm feeling a little light-headed."

"Are you okay?" She pauses, studying me.

"Yeah, just... I think it's from the heat outside and the smoke. I'll be fine. I just need to sit down."

"Of course." She leads me toward the window, and we sit.

"I'm fine. I promise." I pull out my phone and take a photo of the view, then turn and take a selfie of the two of us. I send them both to my parents.

"Are you nervous about going so long without talking to them?" she asks softly, reading my phone screen.

I nod. "It's silly, isn't it? I don't know why I feel so weird about it."

"You'll still get to talk to them when we're at the ports," she reminds me.

"I know." A lump forms in my throat, and I suddenly feel myself on the verge of tears.

I'm an adult. Twenty-five years old. I can go a few days without talking to my parents.

Even though I talk to them multiple times a day, every day.

This isn't the end of the world.

"I'm going to go get us some water, okay? To help you cool down."

"Thanks." I can't bear to look at her, and she seems to sense I need space, for which I'm thankful. Watching your brother die in front of you—*drown* in front of you— and being helpless to save him when you're just shy of three years old brings you closer to your family. At least, it did for me. We couldn't be closer. Couldn't love or appreciate each other more. Throughout our grief, we clung to each other. I know the statistics. I know that typically, when a child dies, the parents split up, but mine didn't. They held on to each other, and to me, like life rafts. Which is why I can't shake the gnawing worry in the pit of my stomach over leaving them, even for a day. If something happens to Mom while I'm unreach- able, if she gets worse, if the unthinkable occurs... I'll never forgive myself.

My hands tremble as another wave of nausea passes over me. I tuck my icy fingers under my legs and rest my head against the window. It's all going to be okay.

It's fine to leave the nest.

Natural.

You're married now.

This is normal.

You didn't have a honeymoon. You deserve this.

They aren't mad at you.

Nothing bad will happen while you're gone.

Several minutes pass before Florence returns with our waters. There's a slice of lime in hers, lemon in mine. She eases down in front of me. "Feeling any better?"

"Getting there." I smile at her and take the drink, sipping it slowly. It's as if I can feel the cool beverage as it moves down my throat and into my stomach.

"I have some sea sickness medicine in my bag as soon as we can get to the rooms. That may help."

"Thanks. I think it's just a bit of anxiety." I pause. "I really appreciate you doing this, you know?"

She squeezes my knee with a playful smile. "I know. I'm the best."

I shake my head. "Something like that."

She laughs. "Hey, so this was weird, but there was a guy at the bar who asked about you."

The statement catches me off guard, and I look over toward the bar, which is crowded with people. "What guy?"

"I don't know. I didn't get his name. He came up right when I was ordering and asked about you. I answered him while I was paying, but by the time I turned around, he was gone. I only caught a glimpse of him out of the corner of my eye."

"What did he look like? What did he ask?"

"He had dark hair, I think, but I can't be sure. He asked if we were together and if your name was Mae."

"What?" I stare at her. "How would he know that?"

"I'm not sure. Maybe he heard someone say it."

Did someone say it? I try to think back. "What did you tell him?"

"I asked who was asking, but he disappeared before I got an answer."

"Disappeared?"

"I mean, it's crowded up there. He was behind me one minute and cut off the next. I thought maybe he came over to talk to you."

"No." I shake my head, scanning the crowd for a familiar face. "Do you see him now?"

She follows my gaze around the room. "I don't think so. He was wearing a yellow shirt. I *did* see that much. If I catch sight of him again, I'll let you know."

"How strange," I say softly.

"Maybe." She shrugs. "Like I said, he could've overheard someone saying your name. Maybe he just thought you were cute."

The teasing grin on her face does little to calm my already heightened nerves.

CHAPTER FIVE

BLAKE

We're seated in one of the ship's dining rooms, our table neatly decorated with a white linen tablecloth and four long-stemmed wineglasses. Mae rubs my thigh under the table as the waiter sets our plates in front of us.

She's ordered spanakopita, while I've chosen a rack of lamb. The waiter fills our glasses with wine and departs, leaving us to chatter softly over the low hum of the music.

"Can't beat this. Dinner and a view, hmm?" Florence says, nodding her head toward the large window to my right. The sun is sinking low into the horizon, painting the sky brilliant shades of red, orange, and pink. From where we sit, we have a perfect view of the water, with no land in sight for miles and miles.

I've never felt anything like the atmosphere on board. There's a sort of freedom here, disconnected from the world in a way that I've never experienced.

"It's beautiful," Patton agrees. "We're going to try to

wake up and see the sunrise, too. I wonder how it'll compare."

"Florence is going to see the sunrise?" Mae asks doubtfully. "Since when?"

She laughs. "Well, special times and all that. How often am I going to get to see the sunrise from the middle of the ocean?"

"Fair enough," Mae agrees. "Either way, I think we'll be perfectly fine missing the sunrise. I feel tired enough to sleep a week."

"Well, don't do that," I tease her, nudging my elbow into hers. "I need my trivia partner for tomorrow."

"Are you guys planning to do that?" Patton pipes up. "I saw it on the itinerary. It looks fun. Mind if we join?"

"Yeah, we love trivia," I tell him. "Mae always wins it for us."

"I want to see some of the live music, though. The Patches are playing. I listened to some of their music before we got here. They're pretty good," Florence says. "And there's a comedy show every night."

"Yes to all of the above," Mae says, seemingly in a better mood. "It all sounds great."

"Perfect. It's a plan then," I say, rubbing a hand on her shoulder. She smiles at me as she reaches for her roll of silverware, unwrapping it carefully and retrieving her fork.

I feel the stares before I notice the man. It's a sort of *knowing* I've felt before. A buzzing near the base of my skull. An awareness that we're being watched. I glance across the table, scanning the restaurant in search of the source of my sudden discomfort. The sun warms my skin through the window, and I turn my head away from the light, my gaze landing on a man four tables away. He's eating with a large group of six other men. They're laughing, apparently caught up in a lively discussion, though he doesn't seem to be a part of it.

Instead, his eyes are locked on us. More specifically, on Mae.

His jaw hangs slack, his eyes as wide as if he's seen a ghost.

I swallow, then look behind us. Is it possible he's looking at someone else? Could I be misreading this somehow? It doesn't seem likely.

"Everything okay?" Mae asks, drawing my attention to her.

I clear my throat, trying to decide whether or not to mention it. "I was just... Do you know that man?" I nod my head in the direction of their table.

"Man?" She follows my eyes.

"Four tables away, toward the back of the room. He's wearing a blue button-down shirt. Tan skin, thick brows. Dark hair that kind of sticks up." When I find him again, he's no longer looking in our direction, but Mae seems to understand who I'm talking about. Her head stops suddenly, and I swear I see her tense up. "Do you know him?" I ask again.

"No." When she looks back, her cheeks have flushed red. "No, I don't think so." She looks back at her plate. "Why do you ask?"

"Because he was staring over here at you." I watch

her, but she can't seem to meet my eyes. Or won't, more likely. "You don't recognize him?"

She looks back over at the man briefly, and this time, he's staring back. He holds her eyes, and there's a look of recognition there that can't be missed. Still, she looks away just as quickly and shakes her head. "I don't think so. He's probably staring at someone else."

The man's eyes bounce to meet mine before he returns his attention to the table and the conversation he's missing.

When I look back at my wife, she takes a bite of her dinner as Florence's gaze dances between us. I want to press her again, but I don't want to make dinner any more awkward than it is, so I decide to let it go for now and ask her about it when we get back to our room this evening.

It's probably nothing.

We're halfway through our meal when Mae pushes back from the table gently and stands.

"Everything okay?"

"Yes," she says, a hand to her neck. "I just need to use the restroom."

"Want me to come with you?" Florence offers.

"No, I'll be okay. Stay and finish eating. I'll be right back."

I watch as she zigzags through the room with determination, around this table and that one, and past a waiter and around the pillar in the center of the room before making it out the oversized doorway and into the atrium. Florence looks at me with an awkward grin.

"How's yours?" she asks, filling the silence as she points to my half-eaten dinner.

"Delicious," I say honestly, though I'm hardly listening as I watch what's happening in disbelief. I spot the man at the far table stand. He pushes his seat in, adjusting a button on his shirt, and then heads for the door, leaving in the exact direction Mae just went.

I take a breath, watching it happen. Of course he'd have to take that path out of here. It's the only way out. But what are the odds? The timing is too suspicious.

I stand from my chair.

"I'll be right back," I tell them. If either realizes where I'm going or why, they don't make it clear.

I rush through the restaurant, between the tables and the crowd, then around the column and through the door. The hallway is bustling, and I immediately lose sight of him. Cursing under my breath, I hurry on. I power walk behind an older woman moving at a snail's pace and do my best not to huff when a group of drunk men bumps into me, hollering loudly at each other as they go, barely noticing I'm standing here.

I spot the signs for the restrooms and zip past the woman, moving along the wall as quickly as I can. The restrooms are down a long hallway, and I slow down as a crewmember steps out of a doorway, his smile quickly fading.

"Everything okay, sir?"

"Fine," I tell him, making my way toward the door.

He probably thinks I've overindulged at the speed I'm moving.

I hesitate outside the women's restroom. For all I know, Mae went back to the room rather than use the public bathroom. For all I know, she isn't here at all. Either way, I can't go inside. Even as panicked as I feel, I know that crosses a line. Instead, I lean up against the wall, tapping my foot against the baseboard.

So much for not being a jealous man.

Jitters fill me as if I've drunk several cups of coffee on an empty stomach.

For the first time, I feel the effects of the ship moving. When I close my eyes, I can sense the shift as we hit each wave with a slow, pulling sensation. My stomach feels too full, my skin too hot.

When the door in front of me opens, I remember where I am. My eyes open, vision coming back to me. Mae stands there, staring as if in disbelief.

"Blake? Are you okay? You look like you're going to be sick," she says after a moment.

To be honest, I'm not sure if I'm okay. I shake my head. "No, I'm fine. I was just making sure you were alright."

"So you followed me to the bathroom?" she asks with a soft laugh. "I told you I was just going to pee."

"I know. I just...you know. I didn't want to leave you alone. I told your parents I'd take care of you, didn't I?"

"Well, I guess I should be flattered." She looks unsure. "Do you need to go, or should we get back?"

"Did you, erm, did you see anyone in there or...on your way?"

Her brows draw down. "Did I see anyone in the bathroom?"

"Yes."

"I wasn't exactly looking to see anyone."

I release a hum under my breath.

She seems to be growing annoyed with me. "How much have you had to drink today?"

"What? I'm fine. I'm not drunk. That's not what this is."

"Well then, who were you expecting me to see?"

"No one. I was just asking."

She stops walking, staring at me incredulously. "You're acting really strange today. Are you sure you aren't feeling sick?"

She's being so casual, and I realize and understand now what a mistake I've made. This is Mae I'm talking about. She doesn't have some deep, dark secret. The man across the restaurant was just a man. She's not lying. I'm the one who's acting out of character. "No," I promise. "I'm fine. Let's get back and order dessert."

With that, I take her hand and lead her back to our table.

We finish the rest of our meal without interruption, and I don't obsess over the stranger.

At least, I try not to.

CHAPTER SIX

MAE

I expected this trip—being on the ship, staring around without any land in sight— to make me nervous, but it doesn't.

Before dinner last night, we joined the rest of the guests and crew on the deck for the Sail Away party, at which point I texted my parents in our group chat a final time to let them know we were leaving and I would check in when I could. Now that Dad's had time to process everything, he's much calmer about me going. He made sure I had plenty of sunscreen and reminded me not to get in strange cabs while abroad, while Mom assured him I was a big girl and I'd be fine.

Most people might be annoyed about their parents being so overprotective, especially at my age, but in truth, it's just our dynamic. It's all I've ever known. Actually, I might be more overprotective than they are. I remind them to take their medicine before bed and call Mom to make sure she's up for her doctor's appointments. At the end of the day, we worry about each other because we know how quickly everything can change. How easy it is to lose someone.

Most people don't get it, and I wouldn't wish for them to. I wouldn't wish for anyone to understand this pain, this fear. Though we all will eventually, won't we?

Still, now that I know they're supportive of this trip, I feel myself relaxing into the vacation more than ever. Earlier, Florence and I screamed along with the blaring music on the lido deck and then we all went for a dip in the adults-only pool.

Today is our first full day at sea, so we're checking things off our growing list of activities we want to do while we're here. After swimming, Florence and I sunbathe and drink by the pool while the guys play virtual golf on an upper deck. We have a quick lunch at the burrito shack, then we play trivia and lose by three points. I blame it on how much we've all drank today— two glasses of wine myself, which is unusual for me. In the afternoon, we watch the band Florence talked about while we wait for dinnertime to roll around, then have another sunset dinner before the comedy show Blake earmarked on the itinerary.

When it's over, Florence suggests we go get more drinks and sit on the top deck. "It will probably be empty, and I think it'll be neat to see all the stars from out there."

"That sounds fun," I say, though when I look at Blake, he doesn't seem to agree.

He stifles a yawn. "I don't know. It's pretty late. I

don't think I can make it through another round of drinks. Can we rain check?"

"Yeah," Patton agrees. "Maybe tomorrow night? We got up so early to see the sunrise. I'm exhausted. Plus, I need to send a few emails before bed and with the Wi-Fi here, it'll take two hours to do that."

Florence scowls. "What? You guys! Seriously? We're on vacation! No work! No going to bed early!"

"I'm sorry," Blake says. "I'm beat. You guys are welcome to stay out if you want."

Florence looks at me with a pouting bottom lip. "What do you say, Mae? Should we make it a girls' night?" I'm as exhausted as the men, and she seems to sense my impending refusal because she quickly adds, "Come on. Tomorrow we'll be in Cozumel, so you know we'll all be exhausted when we get back, and then Costa Maya the next day. And the final night should be all of us. It could be our only chance to have a girls' night."

I sigh. "You're right. Okay, fine."

"Yes?" She beams.

"Yes," I agree, turning to kiss Blake. "Are you sure that's alright?"

"I'll try not to get too lonely," he says with a laugh, though I sense a bit of hesitation. "Just...be good, okay?"

"I'll keep her out of trouble," Florence promises with a wink before wrapping her arms around Patton and placing a kiss on his lips.

I look away. "I won't be out too late, okay?"

"Don't worry. You two have fun," Blake says,

squeezing my arm gently as another yawn escapes his lips. "Call if you need anything."

"We'll be fine. I'll see you in a few hours." I watch him walk away, waving goodbye with a final look and then turn to lock my arm with Florence's. "Lead the way."

PART 2

CHAPTER SEVEN

BLAKE

When I wake up, there's a sour taste in my mouth and my neck is stiff. I roll over, extending my leg out of the covers to cool my blazing skin. Stretching my arms above my head with a low groan, I reach for her.

My hand connects only with the sheet.

The mattress.

Pillows.

Not Mae.

I open my eyes, searching her side of the bed.

The empty side.

I sit up quickly, looking around the room, listening for the sounds of the shower or her in the bathroom.

"Babe?" I call, wiping sleep from my eyes. I tap the phone on my nightstand. It's just after eight in the morning, and there are no calls or texts from her. I panic, trying to remember if she had a room key with her last night, as I picture her locked out in the hallway. It's ridiculous, of course. Our lanyards hold our key cards, and if she was locked out, she would've called or gotten help from our steward.

I cross the room, trying to make sense of my fuzzy memory. There's no light coming from under the bathroom door, but I push it open anyway, checking for her. When I don't find her, I open the door to our room and check the hallway, just in case.

Nothing.

She's not there.

I shut the door and turn back around. Her shoes aren't near the bed, and I don't see her purse anywhere. Is it possible she didn't come back last night?

I push out a long, steady breath and cross the room to grab my phone, where I dial her number. It goes straight to voice mail, and my stomach drops.

Okay. Okay. Don't panic.

I send her a text.

> Did you not come back last night?

We're supposed to have Wi-Fi calling on board, but it's not always reliable. I open the cruise line's app and send her a message that way, too. Just in case this one can be monitored by the company, I do my best to make myself sound slightly less paranoid. Less dramatic.

> Hey. Where are you?

I pace the room for five excruciating minutes, running through every possibility in my mind before I pull on my shoes and head down the hallway toward Florence's room. Maybe the girls fell asleep on the upper deck. Maybe they got up for an early breakfast. Maybe she passed out in Florence's room.

Anything but the worst.

I'm not sure what the worst is... I won't let myself think about it.

I should've stayed with them. The words repeat in my head, berating me. I assume they will until I lay eyes on her again. Until I know I'm panicking for nothing and she's totally fine.

Because she will be, of course.

Totally fine.

She has to be.

When I reach Florence's door, I knock on it louder than I intend to. After a few seconds, I knock again. "Florence?" I call against the wood, trying not to be too loud in the shared hallway.

I hear movement inside, and relief swims through my stomach. When the door opens, Florence stands in front of me with one eye squeezed shut, her dark hair standing in every direction. She inhales sleepily through her nose. "Yeah?"

"Is she here?"

She blinks slowly, obviously trying to understand what I'm saying. "*She?* Mae?"

"Yes, is Mae here with you?"

"No." She gives a small laugh, rubbing her eyes with the heels of her hands. "Why would she be?"

"Because I can't find her."

Her hands drop down and her head pulls back. "What do you mean you can't find her?"

"Exactly what I said. I woke up this morning, and she wasn't in our room. I can't get a hold of her."

"That's impossible. Did you check the bathroom? Maybe she took a shower or—"

"No. Of course I checked the bathroom. She's not there. She's not anywhere. When did you see her last?"

"She... She was..." She shakes her head, thinking.

Behind her, Patton appears, looking equally tired. "What's going on?"

"She was walking back to her room," Florence says, ignoring him. "She walked me to my door and waved good night."

"When was that?" I demand.

"What happened?" Patton asks again, pulling the door open wider.

"Around three this morning," she says softly. "You're *sure* she's not in your room?"

"It's not like it's a jungle in there, Florence. I checked everywhere she could be."

"Wait... What are we talking about? Mae's missing?" Patton asks, catching up finally.

Florence looks at him, biting her bottom lip. "But she can't be... She can't be *missing*, missing. Maybe she went for a coffee or something. Or breakfast. Maybe she was trying to get enough signal to call her parents."

"I tried to call her. I sent her a message through the app. Was she drunk when you got back?" I swallow, fighting back bitter tears as I refuse to ask what I really want to know. *Was she drunk and alone when you left her? Did you leave her to the wolves?*

"She'd had a few drinks, but she wasn't *drunk*. Mae doesn't get drunk. Blake, you have to know I wouldn't have left her if I thought it wasn't safe. She only had to go down the hall a little bit. She'd had less to drink than I had—"

"How can you be sure of that if you were drunk?"

"I wasn't drunk!" she shouts.

"Guys!" Patton cries, holding out a hand between us to silence the impending argument. "None of this matters. If she's missing, we need to report it. They need to search the ship before..." He swallows, meeting my eyes. "They need to search for her. You should go back to your room and call your steward."

He doesn't need to say more. I turn and I run.

CHAPTER EIGHT

BLAKE

I make six more attempts to call her in the time it takes for our steward, Jacob, to reach our room. Florence and Patton pace the small room, sit on the bed, then stand again when there's a knock at the door.

I answer it in less than a second, whipping the door open and staring at the bald man in the hallway.

"Yes, sir." He clasps his hands in front of him, looking official. "You said it was an emergency. Is everything okay?"

"My wife is missing." The words taste bitter on my tongue. Impossible.

He blinks. His eyes widen as if I might be joking. "M-missing, sir? Your wife?"

"She didn't come home last night. We need to call the police."

He puts up a hand, trying to calm me down. "I understand, sir. When did you last see her? I'll need to inform our security director."

"I was with her until about ten last night, but she stayed out with our friend, Florence, until around three this morning."

"I saw her walking back to her room," Florence says from behind me. "We walked back together."

"But she didn't make it back?" Jacob asks.

My jaw tightens. "Correct."

"My room is just a few doors down," Florence tells him. "We'd been downstairs on one of the decks, and we came back up together. When we got to my room, I said good night and I'd see her in the morning, then went to bed. She was walking just a few feet to her room. I never thought... I mean, I didn't expect..." She doesn't finish the sentence.

Seeming to realize she's finished, Jacob reaches for the orange-and-black walkie-talkie on his belt, pulling it to his mouth and speaking quickly. I hear the name Diego and our deck and cabin number.

When the response comes, it's equally jumbled but seems to tell him what he needs to know. He hooks the device back on his belt and nods affirmatively. "Our security director is on his way."

***

It takes about ten minutes before an official-looking man, dressed in black pants and a white button-down shirt with a gold name tag, appears in the hallway. When he does, Jacob's shoulders go a bit straighter.

"Mr. Barlowe, this is Diego Diaz, our security director. He can help us locate your wife. Sir, this is Mr. Barlowe. He and his wife are staying with us, and we can't seem to locate her."

He says it as if I might've misplaced her.

Diego turns his head to look at me, his eyes narrowing slightly. He's serious and intimidating.

"What is Mrs. Barlowe's first name?" he asks.

"Mae. Her name is Mae."

"Okay. And when did you last see Mae?"

He's so calm I feel like I'm going to explode. "I left her with our friend, Florence Hart, last night after dinner." I gesture toward Florence, keeping my voice steady though my ears are practically ringing. "They headed to their rooms at three this morning, but Mae never made it here."

He glances around me, toward Florence. "Is that true?"

She nods.

"And how did Mae seem when you last saw her?"

"She was fine." Florence steps forward to stand next to me. "Tired, but fine. She'd had a few drinks, but she wasn't drunk. We said we'd see each other in the morning, and that was it."

"And where have you already looked for her?" Now he's talking to me again.

"I checked this room and Florence's room and then I called Jacob, who called you."

He pinches his lips with his fingers, nodding slowly. "I see. Do you have a way to contact her while she's on board the ship?" He waves his hands for emphasis as he speaks.

"Yeah, we paid for the Wi-Fi package. I've tried to call her and send her a message, but I've gotten no response."

"Did you try the company app? Sometimes it goes through easier than—"

"Yes. I tried everything."

"Good. Good." He clicks his tongue. "Did you check the dining room? Would she have gone down for a morning coffee, perhaps?"

"She wouldn't have gone anywhere without telling me!" I shout, losing my temper finally. "Why aren't you doing anything? Why aren't we searching for her? How much longer are we going to stand here twiddling our thumbs while my wife is missing? We should be calling the police."

He pauses, drawing in a long breath. "Sir, while you are on board, *I* am the police. I will help you find your wife, but I need to know where to look. I need to understand where she's been, where she might go, and where we should look first. I'm sure this is all just a misunderstanding, and I can appreciate how frustrated and worried you must be, but please, trust me when I say I know what I'm doing and will do everything in my power to help you. Do you have a photo of her, so I can share it with the crew?"

I pull out my phone and find a photo. If I had more time, I might find one I know she'd prefer, but I don't. I don't have time for any of this.

"Thank you," he says once he's helped me locate his phone contact in the app to send it. "Now, you wait here. Call me if she returns or if you get a hold of her before I contact you. There's an option for the security office on your phone." He gestures toward the landline phone on the wall that I used to contact Jacob earlier. "Just press the button. It goes directly to my team. I'm going to alert the captain and crew, and we're going to do a full search of the ship, top to bottom."

"I want to help," I say quickly.

"You can help by waiting here," he says with little room to negotiate. "We have protocols for this. As soon as we locate her, you will be notified."

I step back into the room just before he pulls the door closed and feel Florence's arm wrap around my waist. I let her lead me to the bed, where she sits down next to me.

"They'll find her," she whispers, brushing the hair back from my face. "They will. You heard them."

I nod. I did hear. He'd said *when* they find her, not *if*. It is the one piece of hope I am clinging to.

Three excruciating hours pass, with each set of footsteps down the hall lighting my body on fire, each voice carrying through the walls causing my heart to skip a beat before Diego and Jacob return.

When they do, I know instantly—without having to

look behind them for a sign of her—that she's not with them.

"You didn't find her." I can hardly utter the words.

Diego's eyes fall to the ground, but he recovers quickly, appearing unaffected. "No, sir. We've searched everywhere on the ship that she could possibly be. Every area accessible to guests. We called her name on the intercom system multiple times. She isn't here."

"What does that mean?" It's as if there's no oxygen left in the room. No oxygen left in my lungs. "If she's not here, where is she?"

"We arrived at our port this morning at seven. It's possible she already disembarked."

"You're saying you think she left the ship?" I look around, trying to decipher if it's as ridiculous as it sounds to me. "Without me? She just walked off?"

"Wouldn't you have records of that?" Florence asks. "In the safety briefing, they mentioned they'd scan our passes." She waves her lanyard.

"Yes," Diego says. "We do scan the passes of each guest as they leave the ship. Of course. As of right now, however, we don't have any record that Mrs. Barlowe disembarked—"

"Well, then why would you say that?" I ask, cutting him off.

"We don't have any record, but it *is* possible there was a glitch, or she managed to slip past without getting her key card scanned. It has happened in the past, though it's certainly not common."

"Why would she do that?" I demand. "Why would she leave without telling me where she was going?"

"I'm not saying she did. Only that it's possible. She may have sent you a message that you haven't received due to a lack of cellular service."

I inhale deeply, doing everything I can not to lash out at him again. "Okay, fine. So what now? What do we do next? Have you checked the guest rooms?"

He gives me a patronizing look that says it's a ridiculous request. "Sir, with all due respect, we have a duty to protect our guests' privacy. We don't have the right to search any individual room unless we have reason to believe she's in one."

"But that's ridiculous! Someone could have her! Someone could've taken her!"

"And if we had any reason to believe that, or if we do in the future, I promise you, we'll search the room—or rooms—in question." He pauses, heaving a breath. "Honestly, would you be comfortable using a cruise line if there were rumors the staff searched guests' rooms without permission or cause?"

"Would *you* be comfortable using a cruise line where a person went missing and they did nothing?" I retort.

He rubs a finger into the space between his eyebrows, kneading it diligently. "Sir, I assure you, we aren't doing 'nothing.'"

"Then what are you doing? A search and that's it? You called her name a few times on the intercom, and now we're just going to call it a day?" I dust my hands together, going full smart-ass. "She just *vanished?*

Shouldn't we call the police? There has to be something else we can do!"

"Of course. We've notified the local authorities, who are helping us search the area. The Coast Guard has also been notified and is communicating with any vessels traveling in our direct path to keep an eye out for her. They'll return to the location where we were when we know she was last seen on board—three o'clock this morning—to see if they can locate her. If she doesn't reboard the ship this evening, it will be escalated to the FBI."

"This evening?" Florence asks, whispering in horror. "You're going to make us wait all day?"

"I'm afraid we don't have a choice, ma'am. We have passengers who have already disembarked, and we cannot leave the port until they are all safely back on the ship. Right now, we are doing all we can by communicating with the Coast Guard and local authorities. Rest assured, we will do everything in our power to locate her." He opens his mouth, then closes it again.

"What?" I ask. It feels like he's reciting a script he's been given.

"I was just going to ask... Can you think of any reason why your wife would've wanted to leave the ship without telling you?"

"What do you mean? I've already told you I don't think she would've."

Again, he hesitates but finally says, "Some people look at cruise ships as a means of disappearing, Mr. Barlowe. We just need to know if there's a possibility that could be what we're dealing with here."

"She wouldn't do that!" I shout.

At the same time, Florence says, "That's ridiculous."

The man clearly doesn't plan to argue with us, so instead, he says, "Okay. I will be in touch as soon as we hear anything. I only ask that you do the same."

"That's it?" I demand. "You're just leaving?"

"I can't do my job from inside this room, sir. If you want me to help locate your wife, I need to go back to my office and continue to follow our protocols."

"Okay," I say finally. "What should I do in the meantime?"

"Continue to try and reach out to her. Let her know we've involved the authorities. Update me if you hear from her." He waves for Jacob to follow him as they head for the door. "Don't give up, Mr. Barlowe. I run a tight ship and have full faith in my team. You have the best of the best looking for her."

I can't bring myself to thank him, which he seems to be waiting for. Finally, he shuts the door, and I turn to look at Florence. "She wouldn't have disappeared." I just need to say the words out loud. Just need someone else to confirm what I already know.

She shakes her head, her eyes somber. "No. She wouldn't have."

"She knows what this would do to us. How much we'd worry. She'd never go off on her own, even if she wasn't trying to disappear. She knows how dangerous that would be."

"They don't know Mae like we do. They're just covering their bases." She rubs my arm. "Someone on this ship has to know what happened to her. They had to have seen or heard something. Someone knows where she is."

"And we're going to find them," I say.

She nods, tucking her phone into her pocket. "And we're going to find them."

CHAPTER NINE

FLORENCE

I've never felt so helpless.

We spend the early afternoon searching the ship, walking the same paths the crew must've taken just this morning in their attempts to locate her. But did they look as hard as I would have? They don't know all I do about her. They don't know the way she speaks kindly and softly to me, even after a hard day. Or how she will always choose salty over sweet but sour over everything. They don't know the way her eyes light up when we discuss music or movies. Or that she tosses her hair up as soon as she needs to concentrate on anything at all. They don't know her like I do, and if anyone will find her, it will be me.

It has to be me.

When the search of the ship turns up nothing, I suggest to Blake that we disembark and spend the next few hours of our time in Cozumel looking for her on land. He's hesitant at first. He doesn't want to leave the ship, doesn't want to feel like we're giving up, but I can be insistent. She's not in the dining room, in any of the theaters, in the pool, in the arcade or casino. We haven't found her in any of the bars. She's still not answering our texts. She's going to turn up. I know she is. I just have to figure out what's going on.

Where she is.

Why she's not here.

No part of my mind can comprehend or accept the idea that there could be any other outcome here.

It's impossible.

At this point, I can see why the crew thinks she might've gotten off the ship and, as much as I hate to admit it, I have to wonder if they could be right.

Maybe she's struggling more than we realized and just needed a minute alone.

Maybe she got bad news about her mom.

The thought of her sitting alone crying in a foreign country is enough to break my heart.

So, with that image in mind, the three of us exit the ship through the gangway and make the long trek down the concrete path into the city port. The area is filled with smiling tourists waiting in line to get their passports stamped. Others are carrying their purchased items in giant, colorful bags or grinning in front of the multicolored Cozumel sign that welcomes us to this new place. None of them seem to realize what has happened. No one sees the devastation on our faces.

Every time I catch a glimpse of brown hair, of bright-red lips, I hold my breath. I search for her in every face, in every laugh.

She has to be here.

It just doesn't feel real.

When I check behind me, I realize Patton is staring at his phone again.

"Everything okay?" I ask him, not bothering to hide the frustration in my tone. We stop walking as Blake turns around to see what's happening.

Patton looks up at me distractedly, turning his attention back to his phone at once. "Yeah, sorry. I was supposed to do a call this morning, and one of the new software programs we're developing is... There's a glitch that we're trying to work out, but..." He trails off, typing out a message. "Sorry. I know this is, like, the worst time."

"Do you need to go take care of it?" I ask, but I'm not really asking. If he cared about me at all, he'd see that. He'd realize I need him here. Need him to put his phone away and understand how badly I'm hurting. How scary this is.

"I..." He sighs, tucking his phone into his pocket as he licks his lips and squints his eyes, looking everywhere but at me. "I'm really sorry, Florence. I may need to catch a plane and fly home."

His words slam into my chest like a brick wall. "What? You can't be serious."

"I'm sorry." He takes a half step back from me as if bracing for a punch to the gut. "I didn't plan for it to happen this way, but I need to get this sorted out. No days off for the boss, you know?"

"I'm sorry my friend going missing has happened at an inconvenient time for you," I say with an angry scoff, tears burning my eyes.

His shoulders tense and then relax slowly. "Shit." He scrubs the back of his neck with his hand. "You're right. I'm sorry. Forget I said anything. I'm here. It's fine." He reaches for me, but I pull away.

"No, if you need to go, just go."

"I don't need to. They'll figure it out." Even as he says it, I know he's lying.

I turn back to Blake, and we continue on our walk. I'm not even sure where we're going, only that I need to keep moving. I can't stand still. I need to know that I'm doing something. That I'm trying.

It isn't until I feel Patton's hand slip into mine that I realize he's coming with us. For that, I feel a small sense of appreciation bloom in my chest.

"Where should we go?" Blake asks. "If she got off the ship, where would she go?"

"I don't know," I say softly, chewing my lip. At this point, it's been over an hour since they ended the search of the ship. Four hours since we realized she might be missing. It's starting to sink in that something might actually be wrong. I'm trying to think in terms of what feels safe to tell him and what my intuition is actually telling me. Telling him what I know seems like a betrayal, but if it means finding her, it will be worth it.

I can't lose her.

She can be mad at me all she wants if it means she's safe.

I'll give us just a few more minutes, but if we don't find her here, I'll tell him what I know. I don't like the way panic has started to seize my lungs, making it harder to catch my breath in the midday sun.

"Maybe we should ask some of the shop owners if they've seen her," I suggest, pulling my hand away from Patton's as I move forward to the first store. It's a small hut with a direct path between the front and back doorways. Inside, there are brightly colored dresses, sun hats, and bags.

"*Hola, señorita*! You need a pretty dress?" The man working approaches me in a hurry, grabbing a dress from the rack and shoving it in my direction.

"No," I say gently, brushing it away. "I'm sorry. I'm looking for my friend. Have you seen her?" I hold out my phone, displaying a photo of the two of us at a concert earlier this year.

He stares at it for a moment but shakes his head. "No. No. Sorry. We see a lot of people."

"Thank you." We pass through the store, and I repeat the routine at the next four storefronts, turning down fresh coconut water, sunglasses, handwoven bracelets, and a fish pedicure as I try to siphon information about who might've seen Mae.

We hit dead end after dead end. No one in the immediate area claims to have seen her or anyone who looks like her.

"We should check over there," Blake says, pointing toward a large crowd of people gathered around a pool that sidles up to a restaurant.

"Yeah." I start to follow his lead when I hear Patton clear his throat. Realizing he's no longer beside me, I turn around. He has stopped, staring down at his phone with a worried expression.

I hold in the groan I want to release. "What is it?"

"I should take this," he says softly, looking at me with a gentle expression. "We passed a café over there." He gestures behind us. "I'm going to see if they have Wi-Fi so I can get everything taken care of and focus. I'll catch up with you guys. Go ahead." He starts to jog away, already answering his phone, but stops long enough to offer me a mouthed apology.

It looks almost genuine, but at this moment, I can't bring myself to care. I don't care about anything except finding Mae. Enraged, I storm off toward the pool and the crowd of people. I'm angry that he doesn't seem to be aware of how serious this is. I'm furious that I can't focus on Mae because he's being so awful right now.

I get that he doesn't really know Mae, but how can anyone be so heartless under these circumstances? How can work matter in the slightest when someone is missing?

Once we reach the pool, I force the thoughts away. None of that matters. With a hand over my brows to shield my eyes from the sun, I scan the crowd in the pool. There's a game of chicken going on—two women perched on men's shoulders, trying and failing to knock each other down while a group cheers all around them. Others are ordering food and drinks at the swim-up bar. There's hardly any free space in the water at all. I imagine if these weren't our circumstances, Mae and I would've found a way to get in anyway.

Blake and I pull out our phones. I approach a woman in a lounge chair, reading an Emerald O'Brien mystery.

"Excuse me, ma'am. I'm sorry to bother you."

She puts the book down cautiously, lowering her sunglasses. "I'm not interested."

"No, it's not that... I'm not selling anything. My friend is missing. I was wondering if you happen to have seen her?" I push the phone forward, revealing the photograph of Mae.

She studies it briefly. "No, I'm sorry. I just got here. She doesn't look familiar."

"Okay. Thank you."

I move to the next chair, where a young woman is nursing her infant. "I'm so sorry to bother you," I whisper, holding out my phone. "Have you seen this woman anywhere?"

The woman grins at me, leaning forward ever so slightly so as not to disturb the baby. "I'm sorry, no."

"That's okay. Thank you." I back away, searching for anyone else who looks approachable.

A middle-aged man is watching me closely from his lounge chair, his round belly hanging over the jean shorts he's wearing. Farther down the line, Blake is talking to an elderly couple, holding out his phone. He seems to be having no more luck than I am.

"Have you seen this woman?" I ask the man.

He scoots closer, squinting to get a better look. "Sorry, sweetheart. Ain't seen 'er."

I move down the line, checking with everyone I pass on my way to meet Blake. Most people are kind, and some are even apologetic as they tell me no, while others blow me off. One older woman even swats my phone away.

When I'm feeling completely disheartened, I spot Blake chatting with a man who is pointing and nodding his head enthusiastically. A lump forms in my throat as I jog their way. I need to catch a break. We need someone to tell us something. At this point, it's as if she never existed. No one seems to know anything. No one seems to care. When things like this happen, you're supposed to have police on your side. Family to surround you. Right now, it feels very much like it's just Blake and me in this alone.

"Thank you so much," Blake says, patting the man on the shoulder as he turns away right when I reach them.

I lean over my knees, trying to catch my breath. "What was... that about?" I follow the man with my eyes. "Has he seen her?"

"No," Blake says. "But he gave me directions to the police station in case we need to go there."

My shoulders slump. "Is that what we should do? I mean, Diego said they're already coordinating with the police, but do we trust him?"

"I don't think we have a choice. How are we going to explain the situation? Most likely, the police will just tell us we need to talk to the ship's security team. As far as we can tell, she went missing while we were on the ship. I'm just not sure what anyone here will be able to do."

"Well, someone has to do something! She couldn't have just disappeared into thin air." I check the time on my phone. "There's no way we're going to be able to talk to everyone here before it's time to get back on. More cruise ships keep arriving and others are leaving. This is a nightmare."

"Maybe we don't get back on," he says, pulling me away from the crowd.

"What do you mean?"

"Maybe we should just keep looking here. If she got off the ship... If she's here and we get back on the ship... If we leave her..." His eyes are haunted and glassy when they meet mine. "I can't leave her here all alone."

"But what if she's not here? What if she's not here and we don't get back on the ship, then they find her? What if she's still on the ship and we leave her there?"

"Where would they find her? We've searched every-where there is to search except the rooms, and they've already made it clear they won't be searching there. The more I think about it, the more I realize if she's not here —" He cuts himself off, his body trembling with suppressed sobs.

The truth sits silently between us: If she's not here, then she went overboard. Or someone took her.

If she's not here, she's probably dead.

If she's not here, she's not anywhere.

"No. No. We aren't doing that. We aren't giving up. We won't. She's out there, Blake. We're going to find her. Wherever she is, we're going to find her and bring her home. You know that, right?"

He looks down, kicking the sand under his feet. "I'm trying not to give up, I just feel like we're looking for a needle in a haystack, and I wish I had more answers than questions."

"I know," I mutter, chewing my fingernail. *Okay. It's time. I can't put this off any longer. Wherever Mae is, she's not turning up. Her safety is what matters. I have to tell him everything.* "Listen, I need to tell you something."

As I say the words, the poolside restaurant turns up its music and the crowd cheers. I cover the ear closest to the chaos.

"*What?*" he yells, cupping his hands around his ears to hear me.

"Here, let's move this way so we don't have to shout." I pull him farther away from the crowd, trying to think of what to say. How to bring this up.

"What did you say?" he asks when I can hear him better.

"Here. Come this way." We walk to a small, unoccupied path with a bridge, and I lean against the wooden guardrail, tapping my foot nervously.

"Yeah?" He folds his arms across his chest, waiting. "What's going on, Florence? Why are you stalling? You're scaring me."

"I'm not *stalling*. I'm...trying to put my thoughts together."

"Your thoughts about what?" His tone is accusatory, and I don't like it. I don't like the way he's looking at me.

"I need to tell you something about last night, but I

don't really want to make it a big thing if it isn't." I rush to add, "And it's probably not."

"Just spit it out! We don't have time for this. Mae is—"

"Okay, just... Okay." I puff out a breath. "So, like I said, it's probably nothing. I just want to tell you so it's out there in case... Anyway, last night, after you guys left, Mae and I went to the bar first. We ordered drinks and then headed to the lounge to listen to music. She started to get sad about her mom and I was trying to distract her, so I suggested we dance. And we did. We danced a little bit and..." I bite my lip, pretending to think.

"*And?*" He's growing impatient with me.

Mae, please forgive me. "It's just that... While we were dancing, this guy came up and started trying to dance with her. It wasn't Mae's fault. It wasn't like she was into it or anything. He was just...around, you know?"

"What *guy?*" His upper lip curls in disgust. *Better disgust than anger*, I suppose.

"I don't know. I never got his name. He seemed innocent enough. I really didn't think it was anything to worry about. She's been so stressed since she found out her mom's sick again. And with the anniversary of Danny's death, I thought she could just use a minute to let off steam. Nothing happened."

"Did he *try* to dance with her, or did he dance with her?" he asks.

"They danced together, I guess. Er, well, *he* danced with *her* more than anything. He was flirting with her, you know, but I didn't leave them alone. She wasn't reciprocating. You know Mae. She was just being polite."

"What did he look like?"

I pause. "I... Well, he had tan skin. Dark hair. I...think it was the man you saw at dinner that first night. The one who was watching her."

"You *think*?"

"I can't be sure. I didn't get a good look at him in the dining room. I just remember how you described him."

"Did you ask her about him? Who he was?"

"Not really, no. I mean, I made a joke about what you would think and she laughed and said I was being ridiculous. Which I was. Like I said, it was harmless. I made sure she felt safe, and she said it was fine."

A muscle in his jaw twitches as he looks away. "And you didn't think maybe you should've mentioned this sooner?"

"I did, but I really thought we'd find her! I thought surely she'd turn up and this would be a story we'd all laugh about when we got home. *That time we thought we had lost Mae.* I swear to you, I never thought it could have anything to do with him."

"You didn't?"

"I didn't want to," I admit. "And I guess I was trying to protect her."

"Protect her from what? Me?" He pats a hand on his chest. "How about you protect her from some slimeball who tries to dance with married women?"

"I was right there, Blake! I never left her! I thought it was nothing. I knew if I told you, it would just upset you, and I didn't want that. Not for you or for her. I just wanted us to focus on finding her."

"So, why are you telling me now?"

I inhale deeply, searching for the answer. "Because... Because the more time that passes, the more guilty I feel over not telling you. I still don't want to believe anything bad could've happened to her. I still want to think she'll turn up. And I'm not saying he had anything to do with this, but if he did and I kept it to myself, it would kill me."

He squares his jaw, his gaze darting around. "If you saw him again, would you recognize him?"

I nod without hesitation. "Yes."

He takes hold of my arm and drags me back toward the ship. "Let's go."

CHAPTER TEN

BLAKE

It takes over an hour to board the ship, the line crowded with sweat-soaked people who reek of alcohol and body odor. Babies cry, three men vomit, and two others nearly get in a fistfight before it's broken up. All the while, all I can think of is the fact that somewhere in this crowd, somewhere on this ship, someone knows what happened to my wife.

Once we're safely back on board, Florence and I make our way to the staircase in the center of the ship. I take two and three stairs at a time, darting between people as we move on our way to the fourth floor.

When we reach our destination, she stops me, grabbing my arm. "Holy crap. We left Patton," she says, her eyes wide.

I have to think for a second to even remember who Patton is; I've been so focused.

"Send him a text and let him know we're back on the ship. He can board when he's ready."

She nods, taking out her phone. I can tell she feels guilty, but honestly, who cares? The guy is a total asshole who can't bother to be here for the woman he's with. I say leave him in Mexico if he doesn't care to stay with us.

I look around the room, back on task. I point straight ahead. "Okay. So, when you guys saw the man, it was near the bar in the lounge? That one over there?"

"Yes." After sending the message, she tucks her phone back into the pocket of her jean shorts.

"Great, so we'll start there. Maybe someone who works here will recognize him if you can describe him."

"Sure." She nods and follows as I head toward the lounge. We pass through the casino, and I approach the counter, flagging down a bartender.

"What can I get you?" she asks with a thick Caribbean accent. She's tall, with buzzed hair, dark skin, and a purple nose ring that pulls my attention. Her name tag reads **Adanna.**

"Oh. Nothing, thank you. I was wondering if you could help us locate someone."

She checks behind her. "Who?"

"A man who was in here last night." I look over my shoulder, waving for Florence to step closer. "He was here around…"

"Midnight, I guess," Florence says. "He had on a suit with this bright-orange shirt underneath. He was"—her eyes dart to me as if she's embarrassed—"handsome. Dark hair. Sort of tan. He was drinking bourbon, I think. Something dark on the rocks. He danced with my friend."

74

The woman's head bobs slowly. "I worked last night, but we see so many people..." One side of her mouth draws in apologetically. "Sorry, I wish I could help."

"Is there someone else who might know?" I ask before she can walk away.

She turns her back to us. "Jay! Elijah! Come here."

Quickly, the other two bartenders approach us.

"They're looking for some guy that was here last night."

Florence describes him for them, and the one with a name tag that says **Jay** nods. "Yeah, I think I remember him. He's been in here a lot. I didn't help him last night though. Did you?"

Elijah shakes his head. "Musta been Benny."

"Where *is* Benny?" I demand.

"He has the morning off. He'll be in later," Adanna says.

"Great." I look at the men again. "Did you happen to get his name any of the times you've seen him?" I ask, practically begging them to give me something to work with.

"Nah, sorry," Jay says.

"Would Benny have?"

"Doubt it. We don't really have much time to chat, especially at night. It gets crazy in here once all the shows start shutting down."

"What's this about?" Elijah asks. "What'd the guy do?"

"Nothing," I say quickly. If they're trying to protect him, I don't want them to think he's in any danger from us. "We're trying to find my wife, and he was with her last night. I think they might've known each other. We were just hoping he could tell us if she mentioned going anywhere this morning."

The men exchange glances and shake their heads almost in unison.

"Sorry, man," Elijah tells us.

"I didn't see him with anyone," Jay says.

Adanna steps forward again. "What's your wife look like?" She leans on the bar, suddenly appearing interested.

With a bead of hope in my chest, I open my phone and show her a photo of Mae. "Her hair was down last night, though." I swipe to a new photo. "Like this."

She snaps her fingers and points at the phone. "Yeah, now *her* I remember. She was here. Don't remember seeing her with a man, though. She was alone."

"She was with me," Florence corrects. "But I'm the one who ordered our drinks, so maybe you saw her alone while I was doing that."

The woman shakes her head slowly, studying the picture. "No, I'm sure it was her, and she was alone at the bar for quite a while. Not sure how long. She ordered drinks from me right before I left for the night."

I look at Florence, who seems wholly confused. "No. That's impossible. Mae never ordered drinks for us. It was always me."

"What time did you leave?" I ask Adanna.

"I got off at three. Maybe a few minutes after. She

was my last drink order of the night, if I'm remembering right."

Three. Three was when Florence claimed she was walking Mae back to her room three floors above where we are now. Three floors above where she was supposedly ordering drinks at the bar alone. How could she have possibly been in two places at once? Is Florence lying? Or is this woman? What reason would either of them have to lie to me? I want to trust Florence, and I don't believe she'd ever hurt Mae, but would she help her hide something? She already admitted she wasn't going to tell me about the man. What else is she keeping secret?

"She couldn't have been here at three. We went back to our rooms earlier than that. I was in bed by three thirty," Florence says insistently.

Adanna lifts her brows, her hands up in defeat. "I'm just telling you what I remember. We have security footage." She points to a camera over the bar. "If you want to double-check me, have at it. But I'm telling you, I remember her. She was in here. Alone. At three this morning."

Florence looks ready to argue again, but I've found a shred of hope. If she came back to the bar, for whatever reason, someone must've seen what happened to her. And if there are cameras, even better.

"Everything okay over here?" I catch a familiar voice behind me and turn to find Diego Diaz staring us down. He looks at Adanna as if checking to be sure we aren't threatening her.

"This morning, during your search, did you check the security footage?" I ask him.

He puffs his chest. "Of course we did."

"Did you check it in the hallway? Did you see her leaving Florence and heading back to our room?"

"Sir, this is an older ship. We do not have cameras in our hallways or guest rooms. We do have security cameras in the main guest areas, and they have all been checked. As I'm sure you can understand, certain spaces in the ship become very crowded, making it hard to get a clear picture of one single person. As of this moment, we have not located your wife on any of our security footage."

"Adanna said she was here at three. At the bar, alone. Could you check that?"

"At three? You told me this morning she was in the hallway at three," he says, brows drawn down.

"I realize that. That's what we thought, but maybe the time was off by a few minutes. Could you just check please?" I ask again, equally annoyed.

He looks up at Adanna, who nods. "She was here before I clocked out this morning. I worked till three. Sat right here." She pats the counter in front of her. "Ordered a drink."

"I'll make a note of it and have our team go over the footage of the bar at three." He gives a solemn nod.

"Are there any other updates? Have you found anything? Heard from the Coast Guard?" I ask him.

"I'm afraid not, sir. The Coast Guard's search hasn't turned up anything, and we've received no reports of any ships spotting anything or anyone in the water." His lips press together. "We're actively monitoring the situation and will continue to do so. I'll update you as soon as we hear anything at all."

I want to tell him it's not enough. That they should send lifeboats out, that they should call the police and search every cabin. That they shouldn't rest until they find her and bring her back to me.

Instead, I nod, feeling equal parts helpless and devastated. My mouth is too dry. "Thank you," I mutter.

CHAPTER ELEVEN

FLORENCE

I'm not sure Blake will survive this.

As we sit at the bar, watching for a man who may or may not ever make an appearance here again, I find myself studying him. He seems to be crumbling—imploding before my very eyes. I'm not sure I've seen him have a drink all day. He certainly hasn't eaten. With the blazing Mexico sun pouring in through the large windows, I worry he won't make it much longer if I can't get him to consume something.

I flag down a bartender and order us two waters, pushing his glass toward him. "You should drink something."

He picks it up, swirling the liquid around slowly, lost in thought. Setting the glass down, he turns to me. "She wouldn't have left me."

I'm not sure if it's a question or a statement.

I shake my head, resting a hand on his arm. "She loves you."

He doesn't seem sure if it's an answer.

"Why would she dance with him?"

I press my lips together. "She's going through a hard time right now, you know? Even if she doesn't show it. Mae wants to be okay. All her life, she's had to be the strong one for her parents. When they lost Danny, everything fell on her. And she did it." I chuckle under my breath. "Hell, she made it look easy. But now that her mom is sick again, it's a lot of pressure."

"She told you that?"

"She doesn't have to. I know her. That's why I wanted to do this. I thought the cruise would be a nice distraction, but now..." My words catch in my throat, and I can't bring myself to finish the thought. *Did I do this? Is this somehow all my fault?* "She just needed a night to be free. A night to forget everything."

He nods. "I'd forgive her. I've already forgiven her. Even if she's done the worst. Even if she..." He looks down, pinching the bridge of his nose. Finally, he takes a sip of his water. "I just want her back. I just want to know that she's okay."

I pat his arm again. "Me too."

When someone touches my back, Blake's eyes lock on the person over my shoulder before I turn to face them. Diego stands in front of me, a solemn expression on his face.

"Did you find anything?" I ask.

"Did you see her?" Blake asks at the same time.

He clasps his hands together in front of his stomach. "Could I have the two of you come with me?"

"Why?" Blake stands in an instant, pure panic in his voice as my blood runs cold. Something is wrong. I can see it in Diego's face. They found her. They found something.

"Did you find her?" I ask.

"We have some things on the security footage we'd like to ask you about," he says, then turns, waving a hand over his shoulder. "Come with me."

I check with Blake, who's already moving forward with the determination of an action hero. Set to the Beach Boys music playing in the background and surrounded by people laughing, drinking, and dancing, it would be almost comical if it wasn't so terrible.

My throat constricts as we pass a room where they're playing a murder mystery game. One of the employees is standing on a stage, reading out the list of suspects.

"Charlie Booth enjoys watching true crime on Netflix, drinking white wine, and spending time with his three cats—Fonzie, Momma, and Dylan. He lives next door to our victim and has doorbell camera footage from the night of the murder. Let's chat with Charlie a little bit, shall we?"

The room breaks out into uproarious applause as a man steps up onto the stage.

We follow Diego through the casino, past another bar, and into the elevator. He scans his badge and presses the button for the second floor, which is marked **Staff Only**. Slowly, the elevator moves down, down, down.

When the door opens, this floor feels oddly quiet and

claustrophobic compared to the crowded, sun-soaked areas where we've been spending our time. We are led past several silent offices until we reach one that's labeled **Security Office.** A photo of Diego hangs in a frame next to the door.

Inside, he gestures for us to take the two open seats in front of a small desk with his name placard resting on it. We do and he sits down, turning the computer slightly so we can't yet see what is on the screen when he unlocks it.

"Now, I had my team check the footage from the bar around three, like you asked. As it turns out, we did manage to locate a woman on the footage who matches the description of your wife ordering a drink around three this morning."

Blake looks at me, and my stomach sinks.

"You did?" he asks.

Diego turns the computer around to us, showing us a close-up, pixelated image of a woman's face. It's clearly Mae, despite the distorted quality of the photo. She has a glass lifted to her lips. The time stamp in the bottom corner shows it's 3:17 this morning.

"Can you confirm that's your wife, Mr. Barlowe?"

"Yes. Yes. That's her. What happened to her?" Blake asks, then turns to me. "You lied to me. You said she was heading back to the room." The sentence stings.

"I didn't lie," I promise, trying to keep my voice steady. "I must've gotten the time wrong by a few minutes, but we really did leave around three. You can go back a few minutes and you'll see us leaving."

Diego heads off the argument by saying, "We did see

that. You left the bar together at two thirty-eight this morning. Mr. Barlowe, your wife returned to the bar alone at three ten."

"What? Why?" he demands.

Diego opens another photo of Mae's face from the footage. I try to read her blank expression, try to understand what she must've been thinking. "That I can't tell you. What I know is this: She ordered her first drink from Adanna at three fifteen this morning. Then another from Benny at three forty-five."

"Wait. Wouldn't there be a record of that? Did you guys not check her key card when I reported her missing this morning?" Blake demands.

"Of course we checked it," he says. "That's all part of the process. When someone is reported missing, most of the team searches the ship while the rest of the team checks key card records, security footage and then notifies the proper authorities based on where we were at the time of the disappearance. We also use our intercom system to alert the person that we are looking for them, in case they're just not where they're supposed to be, which is most often the case."

"You seem to have a lot of experience with missing people." Blake's voice is bitter.

Diego remains unperturbed. "We are prepared for anything. For your safety, Mr. Barlowe. Better to be over-prepared than underprepared. Anyway, there were no red flags on her card. Nothing to cause us to believe she was not in the hallway at three this morning like you told us. According to our records, she used her key card to enter your room at two forty-nine. She did not use it to order a drink afterward. After you told us to watch the video, I can now see it looks like she only ordered water with slices of lemon for both of her drinks, from what I can tell. As you know, for water there is no charge. But we did not have that knowledge prior to speaking to Adanna. We were going strictly based on what you had told us and what we could see on her card."

"Wait," I say, sucking in a breath, "so you're telling us she *did* go into her room this morning? When I left her in the hallway, she made it there safely?" The guilt I've been carrying all day is diluted by the realization.

"All we can see is that the door was opened using her key card at two forty-nine. Whether or not she actually entered the room, I can't say. Whatever made her turn around happened quickly. As I said, she was back in the bar at three ten."

"She never came into the room. Someone must've stopped her," Blake says, his jaw slack.

"Well, she approached the bar alone, so perhaps she was just thirsty. This information does help us get a more accurate time line of her actions this morning."

"Why is a bar even still open at three in the morning?" Blake asks, not bothering to hide his disgust.

"We serve alcohol twenty-four hours a day, sir. All due respect, but it's our guests' responsibility to know their own limits." He folds his hands on the desk. I know what he must think of her. Of us. How he must be judging her, assuming there are problems where there aren't. Assuming she's just avoiding us somehow. He couldn't be further from the truth. Mae wouldn't do this to us. She's too kind. Too caring. And she's certainly not irresponsible. I know she's been struggling with her mom's latest prognosis, but I never got any signs that she would do something so irresponsible as to go to a bar alone, even if she wasn't drinking.

Maybe she just wanted to be away from me.

Unless she went to the room and fought with Blake...

I side-eye him. Could he be the one hiding something?

"There is something else you should know," Diego says, interrupting my thoughts. "While Mrs. Barlowe arrived at the bar alone, she was eventually joined by another guest." His eyes dart back and forth between us, obviously waiting for something.

I feel a sinking sensation in my stomach as he turns back to his computer and opens a third photograph. It's another zoomed-in shot of the side of a man's face. The photo isn't clear, but from the looks of it, he's hugging Mae, his mouth next to her ear.

Beside me, I feel Blake stiffen.

"Do you recognize this man?" Diego asks.

"Was this the man she was dancing with last night?" Blake gives me a hardened stare.

I nod, feeling numb. Hollow. "Yes."

"They were dancing together?" Diego seems intrigued.

"Yes. Briefly."

"I recognize him, too," Blake tells him. "He was

watching us from across the dining room while we were at dinner."

"Do you think it's possible they knew each other?" Diego asks. "In the footage I saw, they appear well acquainted."

I don't want to ask what that means. Suddenly, something clicks in my mind.

Blake seems to sense it. "What is it?"

"When we first got on the ship..." I whisper, remembering. "When we separated and you guys went to the casino, there was a man who asked about Mae at the bar."

"A man? *This* guy?" He juts his finger at the screen.

"I don't know. I never saw him. He had dark hair, I think. He came up to me while I was signing for our drinks and asked if that was Mae with me. Before I could answer or turn around, he was already gone."

"Did you ask Mae about him?"

"Yeah, but she didn't see him either. I'd completely forgotten about it until now."

"Could you find that footage?" Blake asks Diego. "From Monday?"

"We can look into it, yes, but I don't think it will tell us anything we don't already know. Whoever this man is, he clearly knows your wife. Though, from the video, she doesn't seem afraid of him."

Blake turns back to the computer, a vein bulging in his temple. "What do you mean? What happened between them?"

"Nothing of note. They drank together for the next

hour and a half. Then, they left *together* around four thirty," Diego says simply. "We lost her after that."

I hate the way the statement feels against my skin. He means we lost her on camera, but we all know we lost her in another way, too. We can't lose her. We must find her.

"They left together?" Blake asks, his voice powerless. He's so pale his skin is nearly translucent. I'm worried he may pass out.

Diego nods. "Do you recognize the man at all?" Diego asks again. "Did he seem familiar to you when you saw him in the dining room? Or to Mae?"

"No," Blake says, "I'd never seen him before. Mae claimed she hadn't either."

"Do you believe her?"

"I'm not sure what to believe." He hangs his head forward, massaging the space between his eyebrows.

"Right." Diego clears his throat, scooting back from his desk. "Well, I'm afraid, for now, those are the only updates I have for you. We're trying to locate the man in the video at this time, and once we do, I'm hopeful we'll get some answers for you."

Blake lifts his head. "You mean he didn't order drinks either? You said they were drinking together. You can't trace his key card?"

"He didn't order drinks during his time at the bar with your wife, no. They both had water, for which there was no charge. We're checking with Benny right now, the bartender who waited on them before they left, hoping he might've overheard something helpful—a name or a clue to how they knew each other, or a plan as to what they were going to do would be even better. We should have those answers soon, and I'll keep you posted, of course. In the meantime, I need to ask you, Mr. Barlowe, were there problems with your marriage?"

Blake bristles. "Excuse me?"

"I'm sorry to be so blunt, but we are spending time and resources on locating your wife, which are meant to be utilized on all of the guests. I need to know if there are problems your wife might've been trying to escape. If you have any reason to believe she might've been having an affair."

"Of course not!" he cries, and the disbelief in his voice breaks my heart. "She's my wife. I love her. We're happy. She wouldn't do this. She wouldn't cheat on me. Whoever this man is...this isn't that." Even as he says it, I can hear the doubt, see the indignance waning. I'm not sure he believes what he's saying. Seconds ago, I would've argued the same thing. Now, I don't know what to think.

Diego taps his fingers on the desk rhythmically, one after the other. "I see."

"You don't believe me."

"I believe what I can see, Mr. Barlowe. What I can see is a woman who lied to her husband and best friend about where she was. A woman who snuck off with another man. Who left the bar with that man. A woman who has now disappeared."

"Exactly! So regardless of what she's done, we need to track this man down. He'll know what happened to her. He's the missing piece! He probably took her to his room. She wouldn't have gone willingly."

"She left with him willingly," he points out.

"She wouldn't... It's him. We need to find him. He knows where she is."

"Maybe."

"*Maybe?*" Blake screeches.

Diego leans forward, lowering his voice. "I hope we find your wife for you, sir. I truly do. But as of right now, we have found no signs of foul play. No reason to suspect anything bad happened to her. We have no witnesses. No one heard anything. For all we know, your wife and this man walked off the ship together this morning willingly, and they aren't planning to return."

Blake crumples inwardly. "You don't know her. She would never do that. She would never..." Then, as if he's just thought of something, he straightens. "She didn't take any of her stuff. Her luggage. Her clothes. She wouldn't have disappeared with nothing, would she?"

"Did she take her purse with her? Her phone? You didn't mention it being left behind, and she had those things in the video." Diego picks up a pen, preparing to jot down a note.

Blake's expression falls. "No. It wasn't... I haven't seen her purse."

Diego doesn't need to say what's on his mind. It's written all over his face. He believes she ran off. He believes we're wasting his time.

"She wouldn't have left her clothes."

"Perhaps she grabbed a few things from your room when she came in last night."

"She wouldn't," Blake insists. "It's... She wouldn't do that to me."

I don't say what I'm thinking—that if she'd wanted to disappear, it would've been a risk to come into the room where Blake was sleeping to retrieve any of her things. Maybe the man stopped her in the hallway, asked her to meet him for a drink. Maybe someone else stopped her... But she was alone when she went to the bar. Was he following her? Did he hurt her? I can't. I can't stomach the thought that it's possible, but I also refuse to believe she left willingly.

She'd never leave us, would she? Never leave me...

When he speaks again, Diego looks apologetic. "Mr. Barlowe, around two hundred people go missing from cruise ships every year. Of those people, most jump or fall overboard."

"Could we check that? Would there be footage?" I ask, my body icy with fear. Is it possible? She couldn't have... The idea of Mae floating in the water as we sail away from her makes my stomach churn. I'd never forgive myself.

"We have checked the security footage. Of course. Yes, but there is no sign of her on any of the cameras."

"Then—"

"But the cameras don't cover every square inch of the space. There are blind spots. It's still possible Mae fell overboard and it wasn't captured on the footage. It's unlikely, but not impossible."

"Why wouldn't you have the entire deck covered? If

you know things like this happen, wouldn't that be important?" Blake demands, his voice cracking.

"We have as much as we possibly can. No security system is without flaws."

Blake scoffs. "Unbelievable."

"The rest of the ones who go missing," Diego continues, his eyes landing on me, "disappear on purpose. They board the ship with the intention of never returning home. They leave at the first port and start fresh with a new life." He pats the desk again. "Cruises make people do strange things. They give them the freedom to do what they maybe thought they never could."

CHAPTER TWELVE

BLAKE

Florence pulls her phone from her pocket and looks down at the screen, interrupting the tension in the room. Looking sheepish, she places it face down on her thigh.

"Patton texted. He's boarding now."

Diego stands. "I'll see you both to the elevator. I should get back to work anyway."

"That's it?" I ask, refusing to join him. "We're done here?"

"With this conversation, yes, but the investigation is far from over. I'm not giving up on locating your wife, sir. I promise you."

"Like you found this clip, you mean? If we'd never gone to the bar and found out she was here, we still wouldn't know anything. You're in charge of all of these people, and you can't manage to find one! *Not even one!*" I pound one hand on the top of his desk. "How is that supposed to make any of us feel safe? How are we supposed to feel like you're protecting us?"

"With all due respect, Mr. Barlowe, I'm not *actually* the police. I'm not a detective. I'm doing the best I can with the crew and resources I have. We're following protocols, notifying the authorities who have better resources than I do. What I—"

"Then why aren't they here? If they can do your job better than you, why aren't they here conducting an investigation? Why isn't this ship being turned upside down until we find her?"

"We've done a thorough search of the ship, sir. Top to bottom, left to right."

"Except you haven't," I point out, my jaw tight. "You're still refusing to do a search of the guests' rooms. For all we know, someone is holding her in their room. For all we know, she's unconscious and—" I cut myself off, unwilling and unable to think of how I might finish the sentence. *Why isn't he doing anything?*

"As I told you, that is not an option. We have done everything in our power, and the rest, I'm afraid, is up to fate. If she were still on board, we would've found her."

"What does that mean?" I demand.

"It means..." He pauses and takes a breath. "It means she has either left the ship or fallen overboard. I'm terribly sorry, but that is just the reality we're facing."

"No." I clench my fists, my chest so tight it feels like a rubber band waiting to snap. "The reality we're facing is that you're going to be facing a lawsuit if you don't step up, do your job, and find my wife right now!"

The small smile he gives me makes my blood boil. "If you'd like to report me for doing what you deem to be an inadequate job, please be my guest, but believe it or not, I *am* trying. I am doing everything I can to help you. For now, though, I need you to leave my office." He holds out an arm, showing me to the door. "I have another meeting in fifteen minutes, and I need to prepare."

With that, he stalks past me and opens the door.

Florence slips a hand under my arm, pulling me to stand. I want to argue, to say or do something, but I can see this is going to be left up to me. No one is going to help us here. If Mae is to be saved, I'll be doing the saving.

He leads us down the hallway and swipes his key card at the elevator before pressing the button to send us back to the fourth floor. Without a word, he turns and walks away. I watch him disappear as the two metal sides of the door pull closed.

"We're going to find her," Florence says, more to fill the silence than anything. "At least now we have a piece of the puzzle."

"Why would she have gone back to the bar? It doesn't make sense," I mumble under my breath. "Did she tell you she was going back? Did you know she knew the man?"

"No," she says quickly, but I can't tell if she's lying. Would she have helped Mae escape? Run away with another man? Leave me? Would she be able to stand in front of me and lie so easily?

I hate to admit it, even to myself, but I think the answer is yes. If Mae wanted to leave, Florence would've helped her. If she needed her to lie to me, she would.

As far as friends go, I've always known Florence was Mae's first, but I've considered her to be mine too, since we met five years ago. Now? Now, I have no idea whom to trust.

"She didn't tell me anything, Blake. I swear to you. She said she was going to bed. I'm not sure why she came back to the bar or why she was talking to that man. I'm not sure who he is. Whatever's going on, I promise I'm just as in the dark as you are... I just want her to come back. I want to know she's okay."

If she's lying, she's a damn good actor.

She glances down at her phone. "I've... I'm sorry. I need to go to the room to meet Patton for just a second. Do you want to come with me?"

"No. I want to do another walk around the boat. There has to be something we missed. Something small. A hair tie. An earring. Something the crew wouldn't have noticed, something we may have passed over this morning."

"Good idea." She twists a piece of hair behind her ear. "You shouldn't do that alone. I'll text Patton to tell him where to find me."

"No, it's fine. Go get Patton. You can join me when you're done." I can't tell her that I just really need to be alone right now. I feel ready to combust and deflate all at once, and being around her, knowing what she kept from me—no matter how small—only makes it worse.

"Okay. Are you sure?"

"Positive. I'll just start out on the top deck and work

my way down. Text me when you're back and we'll find each other."

"Fine. But promise me you'll get something else to drink. Water, I mean. Something to eat would be good, too." She gives me a sad smile. "Mae will never forgive me if she finds out I let you dehydrate yourself."

I nod but make no promises.

When she's gone, I head for the stairs. My mind is racing in every direction.

In theory, maybe I should be relieved to finally have some sort of clue about what happened to her. Instead, I feel angrier and more lost than ever. As if I'm the only one who doesn't know what's going on. As if Mae, Florence, Diego, and this mystery man are all in on something I'm not allowed to be told. As if secret conversations are happening behind my back.

I thought I wasn't alone with Florence here. I thought that no matter what happened, at least I had her to help me get through it—had her to understand how lost I feel without Mae—but ever since she told me about the man, ever since she revealed her lie, I can't help wondering what else she's hiding.

Does she know who the man is?

Does she know where Mae is?

Why would she lie to me in the first place?

Did Mae ask her to?

I think about those things because if I don't, I find myself focusing on the harder questions. Why would Mae dance with the man? Why would she lie to me about knowing him? Why would she come back and have a drink with him? Was she having an affair? Did they plan to run away together?

But how? She had no idea we were going on the cruise, did she? Had she seen the credit card charges, after all?

My mind is a tidal wave of questions crashing into me, forcing me to face what everyone seems to think is the truth: Mae might've left me. Right now, it seems like the most obvious answer. The most obvious answer is usually the correct one, isn't it?

I think back over the past months since our wedding. Almost a year. She's been happy, hasn't she? I've made her happy...

I have to believe I have.

I know my wife is complicated. I know her life is marred with tragedy, circumstances, and emotions I can't begin to fathom, but I've done my best. I've tried my hardest to be what she needs. To keep her happy. Laughing. Safe.

To make her feel seen and understood and protected.

But was it enough?

Was I enough?

I feel like a chump pining over a woman—searching high and low for that woman—who may have left me like an abandoned puppy on the side of the road. Who, for all I know, could be sitting on a beach a few miles away sipping mai tais with a man she might love more than me. Who might not even care about the state she's left me in.

If I give in to that frame of mind, I'm not sure I'll recover from it.

Until there's definitive proof that she's left me, I have to trust my gut.

I refuse to believe Mae left me. I think something is wrong. I think she's in danger. And I'm going to save her if it's the last thing I do.

The top deck, which consists of just a pool, a small tiki bar, and a set of restrooms, is mostly abandoned. An old man is napping with a straw hat over his face while two women read the same book, occasionally looking up at me warily as I search under each lounge chair for any sign of Mae.

The next floor is the Diamond Club, for which I don't have a pass, and then the small golf course. I search the next three decks more slowly. They're more crowded, both with people and things to do. Pools, hot tubs, water slides. Busy-looking waiters offering me drinks at every turn. A track. An open-air movie theater for the movies they show each night. More food. More drinks.

I search for any sign that she may have been here, though I don't really know what I'm looking for. Her purse, perhaps, but maybe something less obvious. A scrunchie. The tube of ChapStick she always carries.

But...nothing.

There are so many people moving about, even with most of the guests still on land, and I can't help thinking that anything to prove she was here would likely have been moved by now.

This is a waste of time, but it's all I have at this point.

The next several decks are filled with guest rooms, but I walk the hallways, listening for her voice, hoping with all hope that I'll turn a corner and run into her. That she'll give me that smile that warms every part of me and say, "There you are! I've been looking all over for you."

The fifth floor is mostly shops and restaurants, but I check each one, getting odd stares from waiters and guests as I go. Most don't notice me, but the ones who do seem certain I'm up to something.

I pass through the library and out onto the deck, checking over the railing. I hold my breath as I look, but to my relief and utter disappointment, there is nothing.

It's as if she was never here. If I wasn't looking, wasn't asking questions, no one's trip would be disrupted in the least.

I turn, looking through the glass behind me and down into the lounge below. From where I'm standing, I can see the bar on the fourth floor. The last place she was seen.

I scan the crowd through the hazy glass. Suddenly, my breathing hitches.

What the...

It's not possible, but it's right there. *They are* right there.

Sitting at the bar where Mae was only hours ago is the man from the photo Diego showed us. The man from dinner. The man who might know where my wife is.

Next to him...is Patton.

I search for Florence, but she's nowhere to be found. How could Patton be inside at the bar when he's supposed to be boarding the ship? Even if he already made it on board, why wouldn't he be with Florence?

More importantly, why would Patton be with this man?

I pull out my phone, search for Florence's contact, and place the call as I move toward the stairs. I have to get down to the fourth floor before I lose sight of them.

"Hello?"

"Hey, where are you?"

"Still in the room," she says, her tone shrill and filled with worry. "Did you find something?"

"No. Er, maybe. Do you know where Patton is right now?"

"Yeah, he's still in line to board. Why?"

The sentence is a gut punch. "Because I was just staring at him. On board. At the bar. With Mae's mystery man."

"Wait, *what?*"

I pick up my pace, more determined than ever to reach them. "Yeah. I was searching around on the fifth deck, and from there, you can see down into the bar and they were there."

"Well, are you sure it was them? You were so far away. I'm literally texting Patton now. He's not on the ship."

"He is." I round the corner and come to the bottom of the stairs. "He's right..." I stop. *No. No.* "He was right there."

"What?"

I shake my head, taking in the empty bar. "I saw him. They... They tapped their glasses together. They were talking." I spin around. "They were right there."

"It must've been someone else, Blake," she says gently. "You were so far away. It could've been anyone. Have you had anything to drink? That heat is brutal."

She thinks I'm hallucinating. That I've made it all up. I spin around again. I know what I saw. They were right...

There.

"Gotta go."

Every hair on my body stands on end at the look on his smug face. I end the call and slip the phone into my pocket.

There's nothing about him that screams *murderer*. No evidence of what he may have done. No scratches on his neck, no black eyes, no bloody lips. Mae would've fought. I know she would've.

He's exited the bar and is moving, alone, across the casino. I have no idea where Patton is, but I don't care. This man is my priority. My only target. I have to talk to him. I move forward toward him in a hurry. A waitress walks by with a tray of dirty glasses, and he stops her. Whatever he says must be funny because she throws her head back with a laugh that has him lighting up.

I take several more steps in their direction before he spots me. When he does, he freezes. The smile on his face disappears in an instant.

For half a second, that's all that's happening. The world around us is still moving, but it's as if everything has frozen and we're the only two in the room. I see the moment he realizes who I am, watch it register on his face.

Then he bolts.

He darts away from the confused-looking waitress in a hurry, and I take off after him, my feet smacking onto the floor with quick steps. My muscles burn as I move; my lungs scream for air as I push forward with more exertion than my body has seen in years. The heat and lack of food or water don't help either. A woman rushes after her child, cutting me off, and I don't have enough time to stop. I slam into her, sending her tumbling sideways.

Shit.

"Sorry! Sorry!" I cry, bending down to be sure she's okay.

She laughs, waving me off. "You're good. I'm okay. Do you see my daughter?"

I quickly help her locate the toddler, then spin around, sure I've lost the man.

Where'd you go?

Where'd you go?

When I catch sight of him disappearing farther into the casino, I set off into a run, but I'm stopped almost instantly by a security guard.

"No running," he says firmly, his arm held out to keep me from moving past him. He's several inches taller than me with a thick chest and large, ropy arms. I'm not inclined to argue with him, but I don't have time for this.

The man is getting away.

"I wasn't running." I'm not sure why that's the lie that comes out of my mouth, but it is.

"Sir, I watched you. There's no running allowed," he

repeats, lowering his hand but moving to stand in front of me.

I read his name tag.

John B.

Security

Security. A new idea strikes me. "Listen, can you call your boss? Diego's your boss, right? Tell him it's Blake Barlowe. I'm the one whose wife is missing. Tell him I've found the man we were looking for. That he just ran through this way. He'll know what I mean." I try to catch sight of the mysterious man again, but he's gone. I've lost him.

I've lost him.

The man eyes me. "If you need to speak with Mr. Diaz, you'll need to contact his office. And you'll need to do that while walking, not running."

It's obvious John is going to be of no help, and I have no more time to think. I shove past him, bolting at full speed in the direction of where the man is headed.

"Hey, stop!" John calls after me.

"Runner! Runner!" another voice calls from behind me. To my right, a guard lunges at me. There's another on my left. A woman at the quarter machine screams with delight over a recent win.

It's pure chaos, but it's over in seconds. I struggle to free myself, but it's no use. Four security guards surround me. One shoves me to the ground while another places a knee on my back.

"Let me go! I wasn't doing anything!" I cry.

"I told you not to run." I recognize John's smug voice from behind me. "You were endangering the other guests. Cuff him."

"I wasn't endangering anyone." The guard who has my hands grips them tighter behind my back, tugging them close together as I feel zip-tie handcuffs clasp my wrists. A muscle in my back burns from the awkward angle he's holding me in. "Please!" I beg as people begin gathering around.

"Get back! Get back!" one of the guards shouts at them, waving his hands to keep people away.

"My wife is missing!" I cry, with no power left in my voice. "There's a man... He knows where she is."

"He's drunk," the guard on my back mutters, prompting laughter from the others.

"I'm not. I swear. Please just call Diego. He'll tell you."

"Come on." The man pulls me to my feet. "We need to get you out of here before the crowd gets any bigger."

I'm dizzy as the two guards spin me around to face the doorway I just entered through. "Please call Diego. I'm not drunk or dangerous. I was just trying to catch the man who was with my wife before she disappeared. My name's Blake Barlowe. You searched the ship for my missing wife this morning."

The man looks at me, something changing in his face. "Did someone call Diego?" he asks, looking over my shoulder at one of the other men.

"Not yet. Working on it."

I feel his grip on my arm loosen slightly. "We'll get

Diego down here to sort this out. In the meantime, you can't be acting like that. People get crazy on these ships. All it takes is one and we have chaos."

"I get it. I'm sorry."

He nods, but he doesn't look at me this time.

"I won't run again. I promise. I was just trying not to lose him. He was also running."

They don't release me, though. Or say anything else on the subject. I've lost my chance. Two of the men continue leading me in the opposite direction of where I was headed. The opposite direction of the man. They lead me through the casino and past the bar, still holding my arm, my hands still cuffed as if I'm a criminal. I remain steady. Patient. Calm.

Embarrassment over what just happened has begun to creep in. I can't help Mae if I'm in some sort of cruise ship prison.

The brig ... Is that what it's called?

I let them lead me into a quiet area that looks like some sort of art gallery, and they stop in front of the door.

"I'm sorry," I say again softly. "This isn't like me."

"Just wait here for Diego. He'll be up shortly."

None of the men speak as we wait for their boss to appear. After several minutes, the sound of footsteps headed in our direction draws my attention. He's walking with purpose, rushing toward us with an air of determination.

"Let him go," he says firmly, waving the men away. The man pulls a tool from his pocket and releases my hands from their zip-tie handcuffs within seconds. In front of me, Diego sighs. He looks as exhausted as I feel. "Mr. Barlowe, you aren't going to make me arrest you, are you?"

"I apologized to them already," I say quickly. "I really am sorry. The man from the video, the man with Mae, he was in the bar. I was chasing him when one of your guards stopped me. I was so panicked I wasn't thinking straight. I just knew I needed to not let him get away." My shoulders slump as I realize it may have been my one chance to find him. Now he knows I'm looking for him. "He was in the casino. You can check the cameras. See which way he went."

"Yes, and if you'd let me know that instead of taking matters into your own hands, I might be talking to him instead of you right now."

"Can you blame me? She's my wife. And God knows what she's going through while we stand here chatting."

He runs his bottom teeth over his top lip, looking away.

"I didn't think. I just acted," I add, calmer now.

Crossing his arms, he nods. "I do understand. But you need to let us do our jobs, Mr. Barlowe. Simple as that."

"Then do them! Why didn't you have someone down here on the lookout?"

Quickly, he folds his arms across his chest. "And how do you know I didn't? How do you know I wasn't planning to get him as soon as he used his card, so I had a name?"

My stomach sinks. "Oh."

"Yes. *Oh.* And now, because of you, we have put him

on alert. Now, because of you, he may not leave his cabin. He may not use his card. If, God help us, he has done something to your wife, you've just tipped him off that we're onto him." He runs a hand over his face in frustration. "Mr. Barlowe, I know you are upset. You have every right to be. But I've been doing this job—doing it well—for more than twenty years. I know what I'm doing, and this will all go a lot smoother if you'll just let me work."

"I'm trying. I just feel like I need to be doing something. I can't just sit here and remain helpless."

He puts a hand on my shoulder, a softness forming in his dark-brown eyes. "We are doing *everything* we can. I promise you. Just sit tight, okay? As hard as it is."

"It's not hard. It's impossible. What am I supposed to do? Go sit on the deck and soak up the sun while I hope for the best? Attend a comedy show? Book a shore excursion at the next stop? What exactly is the best way to *sit tight?*" My voice is louder than I mean it to be. It echoes in the open, quiet space.

Diego inhales deeply, then waves the men away. "Go on. I've got this." Once they've left, he lowers his voice. "We've updated the Coast Guard with the time we now know your wife was last seen on the ship. They'd been looking in the wrong place all morning because of the timing issue. As we discovered earlier, she was still on the ship for another hour and a half, at least, so they've moved to a new search location."

"Have they found anything?"

"There are no updates yet." He eyes me. "Are you

positive your wife never gave you any indication she wanted to leave you? To leave the ship?"

"Am I not being clear about this?" I demand. "No! She didn't want to leave me. We were happy. *She* was happy."

He looks down, then back up, studying my face as if looking for a sign I'm lying. He shrugs.

"What?"

"Nothing," he says. "I just had to ask."

"Again."

"Again," he confirms.

"Why?"

"It is my job, Mr. Barlowe. To find out what happened to her. To protect her from strangers...and from husbands."

My blood seems to turn to gel. Everything has frozen, moving slowly. "You think I hurt her?" I should've known I'd be a suspect, but up until this moment, it hadn't occurred to me.

"I think the woman in the video didn't look happily married. Not to you, anyway. It's my job to find out why."

"I didn't do anything to her. I love her!"

His gaze travels across my face slowly. "All the more reason."

"What are you talking about?"

"Your wife was with another man. You couldn't have been happy about that."

"I didn't know!" I cry. "Of course I'm not happy about it. But I would never hurt her."

"I hear you, Mr. Barlowe. As I said, it is my job to find

out what happened to her, and I'm currently exploring several theories."

"You actually think I hurt her, don't you? Maybe you have this whole time. It's always the husband, right?" I scoff, looking away. "That's what they say anyway, isn't it?"

He nods slowly, done bullshitting me. "Usually, yes."

"I've probably said it once or twice myself while watching the news or reading a book. It's clichéd, but the reality is it's almost always true. *Almost* always." I jab a finger at him. "But not now. Not this time. You've already cast your judgment. I won't waste my time trying to change your mind, but, for the record, you couldn't be more wrong about me. I didn't do this. I love her." My voice cracks as tears blur my vision.

"Get some rest, Mr. Barlowe," he says gently. "And please, no more trouble. I don't want to have to lock you up." He turns, starting to walk away.

"You can trust me!" I call after him. "I didn't do this!"

When I look down, my hands are trembling.

CHAPTER THIRTEEN

FLORENCE

When the door to my stateroom opens and Patton appears and walks inside, he looks as if he's ready to pass out. His forehead glistens with sweat; his salmon-colored sun shirt clings to his body with a vengeance.

"Did you find her?" he asks, rushing toward me.

I stand from the bed. "No, nothing yet. Did you just get on the boat?"

His brows draw down. "What? Yeah. Why?"

I'm hesitant to feel the relief yet. I want to believe Blake, but Patton has no reason to lie. More than that, it's nearly a hundred degrees outside, and I'm not sure that Blake's had anything to eat or drink today. From so far away, through glass, how can he be sure what he saw? Especially when what he saw makes no sense.

Maybe he just needs to believe he saw something. Maybe he just needs a lead. Still, I owe it to him to press Patton harder. Until I'm sure I believe him. "You weren't at the bar earlier? Talking to some guy?"

He cocks his head to the side as if I might be joking. "Why would you ask that?"

"Blake thought he saw you while he was in there." I watch for any signs of recognition on his face, but there are none.

He shakes his head slowly. "Um, nope. Wasn't me. The line was stupid long. I came straight here. Like I told you I would."

"Okay." I brush the hair from my face, then grip the collar of my shirt, bringing my knuckles up to my chin. "He was kind of far away. I told him it must've been someone else."

"Yeah, must've been." His tone is heavy with words unsaid, his eyes studying mine. A pregnant pause fills the space between us.

Up until this moment, I wasn't sure how I'd react to seeing him again. On the one hand, I'm so angry with him for ditching us it makes it hard to want to talk to him, but on the other, I could use someone as smart as he is to help us work through this. Someone a bit removed. Someone whose emotions won't cloud their judgment.

When he opens his mouth again, there's a sort of hesitation that tells me he's not sure how this is going to go either.

"Look, I'm sorry I had to leave you. It wasn't cool. Sometimes I just get so caught up in things, and even though I trust the team, this all really rides on my shoulders. To be fair, I warned you I'm terrible at relationships. This company, for years, has been all I live, eat, and breathe. And I promise I'm trying to find a balance. I didn't have a lot growing up, and if this falls through, I'll have even less and—" He cuts himself off. "But none of that is more important than finding Mae, so I'm sorry. You needed me today, and I bailed. I promise I won't do that again. I'm here. Whatever you need."

"Thank you." They're the only words I can find, and when he touches my arms cautiously with both hands, I fall into his embrace. Tears brim in my eyes as I nuzzle into his chest. I need this. I need someone stronger than me because I'm not strong enough for this.

It isn't fair.

It isn't fair that she's gone.

It isn't fair that we might never get answers.

This can't be real. It can't be happening.

"It's okay," he whispers into my ear, pulling strands of hair away from my sweat-soaked forehead. "I'm here. It's all okay."

"I'm so scared we won't find her," I admit—something I could never say aloud to Blake. "I'm scared I'll never see her again."

He pulls back away from me, holding my cheeks with both hands. "Don't say that. Don't put that out there. We're going to find her. You have to believe it."

I nod, wiping away my tears. "I didn't tell you this already, and you weren't here when I told Blake, but... Mae was with a man last night. While we were dancing. I'm—*we're*—worried he did something to her."

"Wait, what? A man?"

"Yeah. Actually, it was the man Blake thought he saw you talking to earlier. That's why I was asking."

"Oh. Wow." He rubs a hand over the back of his neck. "No wonder you seemed so shaken up."

"Yeah. I mean, I thought it was harmless. They just danced for a little while, same as we'd been doing, but not in a weird way or anything. Just a few songs and then he left. But then we found out she came back to the bar and was with him after I went to bed. I had no idea, and I just... I don't know what to think."

"Well, who is he? Did they find the guy?"

"Not yet. They're trying to track him down."

"Okay, what can I do? What can we do?"

"I don't know. I don't know if there's anything we can do. Right now, I just need to get back out there and check on Blake. He's not holding up well and I'm trying to be here for him, but I have no idea what I'm doing. I'm probably the worst person to have around for all of this because I'm a bigger mess than he is."

"Sure. Of course. Let's go."

He holds out a hand, gesturing toward the door, and we exit our room. In the hallway, he slips his hand into mine. "For the record, there's no handbook on this sort of thing, you know? I'm sure he just appreciates you being here for him."

"Thanks." My voice comes out in a broken whisper as I fight against the sob I feel in my throat.

Downstairs, we find Blake seated on the long, leather banquette along the window in the bar area. There's a full glass of water with lemon resting on the pub table in front of him. *Mae's favorite.* I've never seen him order it. More tears gather in my eyes, but I brush them away.

He doesn't seem to notice that we've entered the room until I sit down next to him. He sits up straighter, adjusting his shirt. His eyes find Patton, hardening.

"It wasn't him." I answer the question he hasn't asked. "He was still boarding the ship. Whoever you saw with the man, it wasn't Patton."

He nods. I'm not entirely sure he believes me, but he doesn't push the issue any further.

"Did you find anything?"

He shakes his head. "Not a thing. If there was anything here, it's probably already been cleaned up."

He sounds exhausted. Fed up. Bitter.

I can't say I blame him.

Still, I owe it to Mae to try to keep him hopeful. To keep him from giving up on her.

I nudge the water glass with my knuckle. "You okay? Sure you don't want something stronger?"

He smiles halfheartedly with one side of his mouth, not bothering to look at me. "It's funny... Mae hates my drinking. If there's one thing we're going to fight about, it's always been that."

"Danny died because some idiots drank too much and plowed into their boat. She hates everyone's drinking. It was never just yours."

"No, I know." He sighs. "Trust me, I know. And I get it. I really do. I guess a part of me always felt bitter about her treating me like a child over it. I felt like she wanted me to give up so much."

"What do you mean?" I ask as he squeezes the bridge

of his nose, his eyes slamming shut to prevent fresh tears from falling.

He looks up and exhales. "Boats, for one. Growing up, my family and I spent every summer on the lake. I gave all of that up for her. Never stepped foot on a boat again. I used to try to convince her it was safe, that I would take care of her." His voice breaks and he stops before leaning forward over his knees.

I place a hand on his shoulder gently. *I'm here*, I want to whisper. *We'll get through this.* But I don't. I can't bring myself to say a word. What in the world could I say that would possibly make any of this better?

Once he's composed himself enough to continue, he goes on, "So, I gave up boating. Just like that, I stopped going to the lake with my family. Sold my Bayliner. It was tough, but... It's Mae. *Come on.* There's no competition over what means more to me." He shrugs, turning his head to look at me as if to say it's obvious. Which it is. "But drinking... I couldn't give it up. She always wanted me to stop, and I'd cut back a lot, but... I could never completely quit. I guess I felt like I'd given up enough for her, you know? I feel like an ass saying that out loud. I mean, I never thought I was an alcoholic, but I really liked it, you know? I liked the way a drink made me feel. And she has a drink now and again, too, so I thought... well, what's the harm? It sounds so stupid." He shakes his head. "Now I can't even stomach the idea of taking a drink." He drops his head into his hands as sobs overtake him, and I lean forward, ready to catch him if he needs me. As his shoulders shake with soft sobs, I feel new tears sting my own eyes.

"Hey..." I whisper, reaching across to rub his back awkwardly. I don't know what to say. Telling him it will be okay feels like a lie. Telling him we'll find her feels even worse. Instead, I say the only thing I can think of, "I'm so sorry. I'm so, so sorry. This sucks."

He looks up as if it's the last thing he expected me to say, and to my surprise, a small laugh leaves his throat. "Yeah, it does." He wipes his nose with the back of his hand. "It does suck." Clearing his throat, he swipes his palm across his whole face.

"She loves you," I say finally. "She does. You make her so happy."

His brows go up skeptically. "Has she actually told you that, or are you just assuming?"

The dry way he asks it makes me realize how much he's doubting everything at this moment. "Yes, she has. So many times."

He leans back against the chair, nodding as if convincing himself of something. Finally, he looks at me. "I need you to tell me something."

"Of course."

"The truth, Florence. I'm going to ask you something, and I need you to swear you'll be totally honest."

"Of course I will."

He presses his lips together as my heart flutters, terrified of what he's going to ask.

"Has Mae ever cheated on me?"

My stomach drops, a boulder sinking down deep in my gut. "No," I say after a pause.

"You hesitated."

"I wasn't expecting you to ask that. I needed to process. She's never cheated. Not that she's told me."

"*Would* she have told you?"

"We tell each other everything."

He scoffs. "Apparently not everything."

"Don't let this make you start questioning what you know about her. We *know* her. She loves you. She would never cheat on you." I twist my lips, studying his incredulous expression. "Everyone has secrets, Blake. But Mae wasn't cheating on you with that man. Or anyone else, for that matter. Whatever is going on, whoever he is, she wouldn't do that. We may not have all the answers or understand why they were talking, but we have to trust that she had her reasons for going back to the bar, for talking to him. For all we know, he was stalking her and she was just being polite. Maybe she just needed a minute alone and he ambushed her."

His eyes narrow. "They were hugging in the picture. They left together. Diego's right... Am I blind not to see it? Not to realize what's happening? And, even if what you're saying is true, even if it was all innocent, what reasons could she possibly have for dancing with another man? Do you honestly believe it was a coincidence? That she blew you off, pretended to go to her room, but actually came back to the bar alone? And then, minutes later, he showed up? Diego said they left the bar together. Is that a coincidence too? Is her not being here all just a coincidence?"

"Oh, so this is her fault. Is that what you're saying?"

"Of course not!"

"Sounds a lot like victim blaming, which is the last thing we need. May as well ask what she was wearing, too."

He groans. "Florence, she's missing. She was with another man just before she disappeared. I'm not blaming her. I'm blaming myself for not asking more questions. I'm wondering if I missed something huge. If I gave her a reason to leave me and I didn't see it."

"You're being ridiculous. Letting Diego get into your head. She didn't leave you, Blake. She didn't leave us. She's..." My voice is shaky as I try to find the words. "She's trying to deal with her feelings right now."

"And she had to do that without me? With someone else?"

"She was just having fun. Nothing happened between them. Diego said they drank water and talked. That's it."

"And am I allowed to have the same sort of fun?"

I flinch at the sharpness of his tone, the self-righteous look on his face. "What?"

"If the situation were reversed... If it was me dancing with another woman, meeting another woman at the bar while Mae was asleep upstairs, would you say the same thing? Would you tell her to trust me? Would you say I was just having fun?"

I don't need to answer him. We both know exactly what I'd say.

He shakes his head, leaning back again and looking away from me.

"I didn't think so. Where is she, Flo? Because if she didn't run away, if she didn't leave me for him, the alternative is worse."

"I know." My voice cracks as I say it.

"If she didn't leave, then someone's taken her. *That man* has taken her. Hurt her maybe. He has her trapped, and we're just sitting here doing nothing." He opens his mouth like he's going to say something else, but he stops himself. "What are we going to do?"

I clear my throat, trying to think. "We... We need to call her parents. They should know what's going on."

He nods. "I know. I've been thinking about it, but..."

"It'll kill them." I finish the thought when he can't seem to. "So close to the anniversary of Danny's death and with her mom sick, it's not fair. They don't deserve to lose her, too. She's all they have left." My eyes swim with unexpected tears for the people I've always considered to be a second set of parents to me. "I'm scared they'll blame me."

For the first time, I feel Patton's hand on my back. I'd almost forgotten he was there, silently allowing us to have our privacy. His palm strokes my back slowly, rhythmically.

"It's not your fault," Blake says.

"Of course it is. I'm the reason we're here."

"We both agreed to the cruise. And neither of us

could've known what would happen. We still don't know what *did* happen. And I don't care what Diego says. I'm going to call the police. See if they can help us. I can handle Bill and Martha, too. I'll call them if you want."

"No. You handle the police. I should be the one to call her parents," I say quickly. "They've known me the longest. They should hear it from me."

His Adam's apple bobs as he swallows, his expression solemn. "Okay."

"Okay," I repeat. I have no idea how I'm going to do this.

CHAPTER FOURTEEN

BLAKE

Time continues to move, despite the fact that my world has stopped.

I don't know what to believe anymore. I'm so tired, yet I can't sleep. I can't eat. Can't focus.

I don't want to believe I could've imagined seeing Patton and the man at the bar, but Florence seems certain and I can't push the issue anymore. I don't want her to think I'm losing my mind.

I'd like to keep myself from thinking that too, if I can help it.

Still, I need to keep pushing for answers and help however I can.

In the safety of my room, I look up the number for the police station closest to our port of departure in Tampa. Is this an emergency? It feels like it, but I still don't think I should call 911.

It takes just a few rings for someone to answer my call, and it's the first bit of hope I've had in hours. I'm transferred to a detective who I'm told can take more information from me.

"Sir? Are you there?"

"Yes, yes. I'm here." The line crackles and she occasionally cuts out, but I can hear her. We're connected. For now, it's all that matters.

"I'm Detective Jenkins. Can you tell me what's going on?"

"My name is Blake Barlowe. I'm on a cruise ship right now. We're at our first port of call in Cozumel. When I woke up this morning, my wife wasn't there. I've reported her missing to the security director and they've searched the ship, but they're refusing to do anything else. There's a man who was with her last night at the bar, and according to the security team, they left together, but—"

"Do you know the man?"

"I don't. They aren't telling me anything. I'm worried he's taken her or hurt her, and I'm stuck on this boat. They say the Coast Guard is supposed to be looking into it, but I'm not getting any real updates. I know time is of the essence, and I just... I just want to find her."

"Sir, you're cutting out a little, but I think I got most of that. What time were you last with your wife?"

"I was with her last night, but she stayed out with a friend of ours until early morning. They have her on the security footage with the man at the bar until four thirty."

"The man is your friend? I thought you said you didn't know him?"

"No, I don't. Our friend is a woman, Florence. They

were together until about three. Then Florence went to bed and Mae stayed."

"I see. And where were you when your wife was last seen?"

"I was in bed."

"No, sorry. I meant, where was the ship?"

"Oh... Um, I'm not sure. Should I know that?"

"I thought your security director might've told you. What time did you arrive at your port of call?"

"Uh, seven, I think."

"So you would've been in international waters." She sucks in a breath. "Okay, look, I can take down this information, but unfortunately, until you're back on US soil, you're out of our jurisdiction."

"But we're American citizens!"

"I know. I get it, but right now, our hands are tied. The second you're back, I'm happy to meet with you and take your statement and see what we can do. If the Coast Guard is already involved, it sounds like you're in good hands." Her voice changes when she speaks again. It's softer somehow. "I know you have to feel helpless, but you did the right thing by calling. Just try to stay positive, okay? And if she hasn't turned up by the time you arrive back here in Florida, we'll do our best to help you locate her."

"Thanks," I say softly. I've never felt so helpless. Brick wall after brick wall, I just keep slamming into dead ends. Is this really all that can be done? Are they really doing everything?

Why doesn't anyone care about Mae? Why don't they know how special she is?

Why can't they see that the world is a little dimmer without her? That we all need her back? That we have to find her?

She ends the call and I exit the room, my shoulders slumped, my body sore.

I find Florence on the top deck, looking out over the port. She looks as terrified as I feel, eyes narrow and searching the crowds below.

I move to stand next to her, and when she looks at me, it's with a breath of hope that quickly disappears.

"What did they say?"

I shake my head, my voice trembling as I answer. "They... Uh..." I choke back an angry sob. "We're on our own, Flo. They can't help until we're back in Florida and the crew can't help until everyone's back on the ship, but even then... It's just us. No one else cares. No one else is doing anything." I gesture around, past the crew milling about with trays of drinks for the passengers who remain on the ship, past the toddlers splashing in the splash pad with their happy parents watching from nearby, past the older couple posing for a picture with the ship's photographer.

She nods as if she hasn't been expecting anything different. "Her parents didn't answer." She pulls a bit of hair from her mouth. "I tried both of them and left a message for Bill to call me."

I drop my head forward. "What are you going to tell them?"

She grips the railing with both hands. "That we're doing everything we can. That we won't give up until we find her."

"Until she's safe," I add. I need to keep saying it. To keep hearing it. I need it to be true.

She reaches over and strokes my arm gently. "Until she's safe."

The afternoon rolls into the evening and the evening into the night. And when Florence won't take no for an answer—won't shut up about how I need to rest, how Mae would want me to rest, how I'm no use to anyone if I'm so tired I can't keep my eyes open—I end up back in my room. In the bed I'm meant to share with Mae.

Her absence is loud.

Pronounced.

Her clothes are here. Her perfume. Her hair products and face creams. I can't bring myself to touch anything, as though if I were to leave it all just as she had it, she might walk back in the door and just resume where we left off.

My body physically aches from missing her. I didn't know that was possible. I feel like I'm being compressed, as if I'm in a room where the walls have closed in, pressing on me from every side. Breathing is painful. I close my eyes, but I only see her. Hear her.

I try to think back over our last interactions. The look on her face. Our last conversations. What did I miss? Did she try to tell me something was wrong? Were there any hints this was coming?

As I remain in the dark, both in the literal and metaphorical sense, new ideas hit me. Diego mentioned that some of the disappearances were from people jumping or falling overboard. Could she have...

I don't even want to consider it, but I must. At this point, the ship is on course. All the passengers have reboarded and been accounted for, and Diego informed me Mae wasn't one of them. If she left the ship with the intention of not getting back on board, not returning to me, it worked. But her key card wasn't scanned to leave the ship, according to the security team. Which means she either slipped past the crew somehow while disembarking—which seems unlikely—or she's still on the ship —which is still my most prominent theory, that someone has her, that the man has her—or she left the ship through other means. Which brings me back to the theory she may have jumped or been pushed.

Would she have jumped? I know Mae has been going through a lot lately, but could I really have missed something as big as that? There were no signs. I'm sure of it.

I feel heavy with grief but also angry with myself for grieving. She may come back. She may still need me to fight for her. Not to give up.

I'm in such a weird sort of limbo, not knowing anything. As we pulled away from the shore earlier, my heart ached so badly at the thought of leaving the place she may still be. If we don't find her, I'll always wonder if I should've stayed. If I should've searched all of Cozumel for her, demanded help from the authorities, but where would I have even started? But if I did get off and she was still on the ship, where would that have left us?

If I could tear myself in half for her, be in two places at once, I would.

I'd do anything for her, and that makes me bitter too, because what if she chose to leave me? I haven't been perfect, maybe, but I don't deserve this. If she left me, I'll never be able to forgive her.

Of that, I'm certain.

I squeeze my eyes shut, begging the universe, selfishly, for a moment of peace in the form of sleep. For the pain to stop long enough for me to rest.

My request is firmly denied in the form of a knock on the door.

I jolt. It might be her. I swear my heart almost stops completely as I stand and cross the room in a second. I swing the door open, holding my breath, and freeze.

The woman in my doorway is not the one I expected to see.

"Florence?"

"I know it's late," she whispers, glancing behind her. "I figured you weren't sleeping either."

"Not a wink," I say gently, stepping back so she can enter the room. I want to ask if everything's okay, but regardless of why she's here, we both know it's not.

She spins around to face me when I shut the door, and we're trapped in the small hallway in front of the bathroom. Her next sentence makes the space feel even smaller. "Bill finally called me back. They were in doctor's appointments all day."

I nod. I knew he'd eventually return her call, but I'd hoped they'd be busy and he'd wait a few more days. Until we were back in Florida. Until we knew more. "How'd they take it?"

"I mean, not well. They're devastated, obviously. I could hardly understand them through the tears. They're coming down to meet us at the port. Martha can't fly, so they have to drive, which makes it even worse. I think they were leaving before we even got off the phone. Mae would hate to know they're driving this far. Bill promises they'll drive nonstop as long as Martha can make it, but I told them to do what they can. I promised them we'd wait."

"Of course." I'm not sure I plan to leave Florida ever. To leave would feel like giving up on her.

"I don't think any of us will survive this," she says gently. It's maybe the most honest thing either of us has said all day.

"Me either."

"I don't know if I want to." She leans forward, wrapping me in a lingering hug that feels like she needs it as much as I do.

I want to tell her she doesn't mean that. That, of course, she wants to survive. But I don't say anything. It would be hypocritical because the truth is, the more I contemplate life without Mae, the more I'm inclined to agree with her.

"I should get back," she whispers before pulling away. "Try to sleep, okay?"

"I will." It's not a lie. I'll try. I'm just sure it won't happen. "You too."

I catch the reflection of the light from the hallway on her tear-stained cheeks when she pulls the door to the hallway open. With that, she's gone, and I'm left utterly alone again.

I'm haunted by the silence, by the lack of her.

CHAPTER FIFTEEN

FLORENCE

When I get back to my room, Patton is still asleep with his noise-canceling headphones on, and I'm certain he didn't realize I ever left. It's not his fault, I know, but I can't help feeling angry at him again. It must be nice to sleep so soundly while I feel like my life is falling apart.

He's trying, I guess, but it's not enough. I'm not sure what would be, but this...this is not enough. On the night-stand, his phone is buzzing. That noise has begun to cause a headache to form at the base of my skull when-ever I hear it, which is often. For once, though, it continues to ring as he sleeps through it.

I'm not sure how to do this.

Without Mae, I'm not sure who I am. She took me in during our senior year of high school when I was the new kid in town and had no interest in making friends. From that moment, we've been inseparable. She's supposed to be in my wedding. She's supposed to spoil my kids.

How am I supposed to do any of this without her?

Earlier, when Blake said it would be worse if she hadn't left willingly because it meant someone had taken her, I could never tell him what I was thinking. I could never tell anyone. I know how selfish it is. How terrible it makes me. But I can't help thinking her leaving *would* be the worst. If someone has taken her, it means she didn't have a choice. If she purposefully left me, thought it through and made the choice to never see me again, to live the rest of her life without me, I'm not sure how to stomach that.

I don't know how to accept that version of my best friend. One who could see me as so easily dispensable.

I make my way across the room slowly when the buzzing from Patton's phone finally ceases. I'm guessing it will just be a few more minutes before it starts up again. I kick off my shoes and grab a hair tie to pull my hair up but freeze when I hear something out in the hallway.

Footsteps.

Most likely, it's someone in a room next to ours. I tie my hair into a messy bun atop my head and reach for the covers.

There it is again.

It sounds like someone is standing just outside the door. Pacing, maybe. I move back from the bed and turn around, returning to the small hallway in front of the bathroom. Maybe Blake followed me back to the room. I check my phone to be sure there are no missed texts from him before I step forward toward the door, ease the peephole cover over, and peer out into the hall. To my surprise, I see a familiar face, though not the one I was expecting.

What is he doing?

Diego stands outside, staring at the door intently. I'm torn between the desire to rip it open and demand to know what he's doing or continue watching and see what happens. Luckily, I don't have to decide because as quickly as the thought comes, I watch him lift his hand and knock softly on the door. I feel the vibration of it against my chest.

Sucking in a breath, I pull the door open.

"What are you doing here?"

He folds his hands in front of him, shoulders squared. "I'm sorry it's late. I called your room, but there was no answer."

"I..." I glance at the phone behind me on the wall. "I stepped out for a minute. I must've missed your call." Had Patton really slept through that, too? "Is something wrong?"

"I need to talk to you," he says. "It's urgent. Can you come with me?"

I swallow, checking in with my gut. I don't know or trust this man, but he could be the key to finding Mae. I step back. "Actually, I'd prefer it if we talk here."

He tilts his head, looking behind me to where Patton is sleeping on the bed. "Won't we disturb him?"

"It's fine. What's going on?"

He inhales deeply, preparing himself. "We located the man who was last seen with Mae."

My throat constricts. "You did?" *Does this mean they found her? Is she okay? Is she...not?*

"We did. One of the staff spotted him in the dining room during dinner, and we were able to track his card to get his room number. I just finished talking to him. He also allowed us to search his room."

"And? What did he tell you? Did you find her?"

"Mae was not in the guest's room, nor were there any signs she had been there, but we did question him about his involvement with her. He was very cooperative."

"What did you find out?" I demand. He's withholding information, making me pry it out of him, and I can't decide if it's because he's trying to determine how much to share or because he's enjoying holding power over me.

"The gentleman told us that he and Mae were acquaintances. To put it frankly, he said they'd been romantically involved." He's being so proper now I have to assume the man gave them intimate details of their supposed romance. It's ridiculous. I don't want to believe it. Of course he'd say that.

"That's...absolutely insane. He's clearly lying."

"I don't think so, Miss Hart. He seemed to be very sincere in his concern for her."

"If they'd dated, I'd know. What is his name?"

"His name is Zach Carter. He lives in Tampa and claims to have spent time with Mae Barlowe—then Mae *Leighton*—over the course of many summers during their adolescence. He knew her quite well, from what he told me." I barely register that he has pronounced her maiden name correctly—*Lee*-ton—despite how often it's mispro-nounced as *Lay*-ton, which makes it more likely he actu-ally spoke to someone who knew her.

It doesn't matter, though. I'm no longer listening. Not really. Instead, my mind short-circuits as soon as he says Zach's name.

"I know him," I blurt out.

"Excuse me?"

"Zach Carter. He's telling the truth. He and Mae..." I pause, recalling the many conversations we've had revolving around Zach. He was her ongoing summer rela-tionship every year when they came back to honor Danny's memory. They knew each other as young kids and grew into awkward teens. She loved him once. He'd been her first kiss. The first boy she ever had sex with. Why hadn't she told me that was him? Why hadn't I recognized him from the pictures she's shared with me? Then again, it's been years since they saw each other, years since she had any pictures of or with him. "She loved him," I say softly, meeting his eyes. I don't want to say out loud what I'm slowly realizing. If there was ever anyone Mae would leave Blake for, it would be Zach.

"I get the feeling that was reciprocated. Is it possible they were carrying on an affair?"

"No," I say, though I can feel the insincerity seeping into my veins. Truth is, I don't know. Minutes ago, I would've wholeheartedly said no. I would've said there was no way Mae would have an affair and not tell me, not confide in me. But now? Now, I'm not sure what to think. How could she have not told me that Zach was on this ship? That Zach was the one she was dancing with? The one she was talking to when I walked away to get us something else to drink. What else was she hiding from me? From Blake?

"Perhaps Zach was interested in resuming their relationship, but Mae turned him down?"

I waver, trying to comprehend everything I'm learning. "Is that what he told you?"

"No. He said he walked her back to the elevator after they left the bar. That he hasn't seen or heard from her since."

"Okay, so why are you telling me this? Why not tell Blake?"

"How do you know I haven't already told this to Blake?"

"I was just there," I say before I've had time to think it through.

Diego's brows draw down, his mouth opening, then closing quickly.

"I mean, I was just in Blake's room to check on him. Before I came here. He didn't mention anything, and you wouldn't have had time to go there and tell him all of this before you got here."

"You're right. I haven't told him yet."

"Why?"

He presses his lips together, his eyes darting across my features, reading me.

"Why?" I ask again with more force.

"I've already told you one theory. Maybe Zach pursued Mae and she turned him down. Maybe that made him angry and he hurt her in some way... But my other theory is a bit more complicated."

"Because?"

"What if she didn't say no? What if they left the bar and something happened between them? And what if, after that, Mr. Barlowe found out about it? Or what if she woke him up when she came to the room that night and he followed her and saw them together?"

"He would never have hurt her," I mutter breathlessly, running his words through my head again.

"Mrs. Barlowe left the bar with Zach Carter at just after four thirty in the morning. It wasn't until just before nine that we were notified of her disappearance. That's plenty of time for something to have happened, for her to have gone back to her room to be confronted by her husband, and for him to have lashed out."

"Lashed out, as in killed her?"

He doesn't nod, but he doesn't need to.

"No. No, that's ridiculous. Impossible. You don't know them. Blake is... He's not like that. He's not jealous. He's patient. And you haven't seen him today. He's completely broken over this."

"Could he not be completely broken over what he did?"

"I'm telling you, you've got it wrong."

"Maybe I do. I've been wrong before. I'll be wrong again. But for now, Miss Hart, until he proves me wrong, I don't think I am."

"He loves her."

"All the more reason."

I shake my head, backing away as if to distance myself from the theory. "I get how this looks, but he didn't do this. There's no way he's this good of an actor. I've been with him all day. I would know. I would sense it. Whatever happened, Blake wouldn't do this."

He gives me a look full of pity. "All I'm saying is that you should be careful. Try not to spend too much time with him alone. We never know what people are capable of."

Well, that much, I'm learning, is certainly true.

Once he leaves my room, I check to see that Patton is still sleeping peacefully as I process what I've just learned. Zach Carter, the boy my best friend first loved, who grew into a man, is not only on this ship, he was the last person to see her before she disappeared.

The two most likely suspects in her disappearance are Zach and Blake. It's just a fact.

I consider Blake to be one of my best friends. I'd trust him with my life. My darkest secrets. I don't believe he's capable of this, but I need to prove it. Which means I need to tell him what I know.

I leave the room and rush down the hallway, hoping I'm not making a terrible mistake when I knock on his door again. It takes him several minutes to open the door, and when he does, his hair is disheveled, his eyes blood-shot. He's been crying again.

"Hey, I need to talk to you."

"Yeah. Sure. Just...give me a sec." He darts into the bathroom and flicks on the light, shutting the door behind him seconds before I hear him start to vomit. I walk away from the door, stepping near the bed to give him as much privacy as possible.

On the small vanity in front of the mirror are tiny bottles of her beauty products. I pick one up, lifting it to my nose. It's a face cream we discovered accidentally while looking for something else in Ulta. When the beauty associate recommended it, she told us it smelled like candy.

I can still remember the way Mae giggled when she squirted a small drop onto her fingers and sniffed. *"Oh my god, it really does!"* She'd pushed her hand forward to let me smell at the same time I'd leaned in, and it smeared across the end of my nose, sending us both into a fit of laughter.

Now, the scent brings tears to my eyes. I place it down and take in the rest of the room. It's still neat and proper, a sign that Blake hasn't touched much since Mae was here. He's always been a little bit messier than her. It drove Mae crazy the way he would use kitchen towels and lay them on the counter instead of hanging them back up or how his shoes were always sitting wherever he'd taken them off rather than put away in the closet.

If this room just belonged to Blake, it would be much less neat, that's for sure.

Curiosity blooms in my stomach as Diego's warnings repeat in my head. I carefully comb over each of her things, looking for any signs that things are amiss. I check the trash can next, but it's empty, cleaned up by the room steward.

I bend down, running my hands under the edge of the bed, when I hear the toilet flush.

My hand connects with something soft, and I freeze. Pulling it out, I run my hands over the fabric in disbelief. It's not possible.

It can't...

He wouldn't.

No.

No.

No.

The door opens behind me while I'm still frozen in place, staring at the damning piece of evidence in my hand.

"What are you doing?"

I turn my head to look at him. "What did you do?"

CHAPTER SIXTEEN

BLAKE

Florence stands up, holding one of Mae's dresses in her hand.

"What do you mean what did I do?"

"Why is this here?" she demands, staring at me as if I'm a stranger. Worse, as if I'm a monster. I can still taste the vomit on my tongue; the sting of it still burns my throat. Apparently, not only am I not going to be able to eat with Mae gone, but I'm also not going to be able to keep what little I *do* eat down.

"Sorry." She's still waiting for me to respond. I study the dress in her hand. "Um, I don't know. Where was it?"

"On the floor under the bed," she says.

"She must've dropped it. It probably got shoved out of the way. Why?"

"Blake, what did you do?" she asks, shaking her head in horror.

Every hair on my body stands. "What do you mean? Why are you looking at me like that?"

"You have to tell me." Her voice cracks. "Why do you have this?"

"Her dress? Why wouldn't I?"

"Not just any dress." She shakes it at me. "This was the dress she was wearing when she disappeared."

My muscles clench. *Is this a joke?* "*What?* No."

Her chin rises and falls. "Mae was wearing this at the bar with me last night."

"No. That's impossible." I try to think back over yesterday, but my memory is such a blur. I'd had too much to drink, I was exhausted, and I'm not one to care about what she's wearing anyway. "No."

"Yes." Her tone is firm. Certain. "This was what she wore. How would it have gotten here?"

"I don't know."

"That's not a good enough answer."

"What do you want me to say? I swear to you, I don't know how it got here." I run a hand through my hair and over the back of my neck. "She... She came back here, right?"

"You said she didn't come in the room!"

"I said I never woke up if she did. Maybe she snuck in and changed."

But why? I can't ask her the question. Without saying a word, she's the one asking me. Why would she have come back and changed only to leave again? Was it before she went to the bar? Or after? Briefly, I imagine my wife slipping into the room and putting on a disguise, leaving under the guise of being someone else. It's as if I don't know her at all. My stomach clenches, threatening to erupt again. "Florence, look at me."

Her brown eyes meet mine, wild and feral. She's an animal, and I have her trapped. I step to the side, giving her a clear path to the door to make myself less of a threat. I need her to hear me. My hands go up near my face, bouncing up and down slowly as I speak.

"I didn't hurt Mae, okay? You know that. But if that dress is here, it means *she* was here at some point, right? That's a good thing! She could've been in here today, even. It could mean she's still on the ship, couldn't it?"

She glances down at the dress, gripping it tightly. "No, this has to be from last night. If she came into the room again, Diego would've seen it on her key card. When she came back here last night, when I left her in the hallway, she must've changed then. What was she wearing in the photographs Diego showed us? From the bar?"

"No. That doesn't make sense. Why would she have changed just to go back down to the bar? It had to be *after* that. I'm telling you, this is a sign! Maybe a steward let her in."

"No, Blake. Stop. Stop and think. What was she wearing at the bar with..." She hesitates, stopping herself from saying something else.

I don't want to think about that. Don't want to think that this isn't proof she's still alive. Still here. It's the first piece of hope I've had all day. I need to believe this means she's still here.

"She had to have changed *before* she went down to

the bar last night. When Diego said she used her key card to enter the room," Florence says finally.

"No." I shake my head. "No." I can't picture it. Can't imagine her slipping into the room, past my sleeping form, changing, and leaving again. Can't believe she could look at me and still go through with her plan to sneak to the bar alone, to potentially meet another man.

Maybe she was in here today.

Maybe while I was searching all over the port of Cozumel for her. Or while I was nearly getting arrested in the casino.

As I replay my day, hope is replaced by anger in my chest. *How could she do this to me?*

"We have to tell Diego," she says, her voice barely above a whisper. "He has to know that we found this. We have to ask him what she was wearing in that video. Now that I'm thinking about it, we only saw shots of her face. I couldn't see what she was wearing. Getting that answer will help us narrow down *when* she was here."

I almost agree, but stop myself, worry pooling in my gut. "I don't know if that's a good idea."

"What are you talking about?" She looks up at me.

"What will it look like if we tell him about this?" I think through the words as I say them, more convinced than ever that I'm right. "He'll assume the same thing you did. This dress being here makes me look guilty, even to you. You know me, Florence. You know how much I love her. You know I wouldn't do this, and you still questioned it. But he doesn't. He already thinks I'm guilty. Maybe the entire crew does. He already thinks we had marital problems. That I hurt her or she left me. Either way, if we show this to him, it'll just make things worse."

She twists her lips in thought, and I silently will her to agree with me, to hear what I'm saying. "What if she left you for him, Blake?"

"She left me, yet he's still on the boat? I saw him earlier, Florence," I remind her, though I know she still thinks I hallucinated the whole thing. "They didn't leave together. He's still here."

"*What will you do?*" she presses, her voice firm and slow.

"What can I do?" I ask with a groan. "At this point, there's nothing to be done if that's what she wants. Will it absolutely destroy me? Yes. But at the end of the day, I just want to know that she's safe. As much as it'll kill me, to know she's okay would be enough for now."

"Okay. Because I need to tell you something else."

I feel the weight of her words as they swell and fill the room. There's hardly any space for the two of us in here anymore.

"What?" I'm not sure I can take any more reveals.

"Do you know the name Zach Carter?" She studies my face as she asks the question.

Something about it does ring a bell, but I'm unsure of why. "It sounds familiar, maybe. Should I?"

"Possibly... He's the man who was with Mae at the bar, the one who danced with her, who saw her across the dining room. I'm convinced he's the man who asked me about her when we first boarded."

"How do you know that? Why are you just now

telling me? Do you know him?" I demand as the floor seems to shift underfoot. Was this another secret? Another lie?

"I just found out. And no, I don't know him, but I know *of* him. Diego came to my room a few minutes ago to tell me they tracked him down, and I recognized the name. He swears he didn't do anything and they searched his room, but..."

"But?"

"They used to date, Blake. They were in love, from what I know. I hadn't heard her talk about him in years. I don't think they were having any sort of affair. But you deserve to know the truth, so there it is."

"There it is..." I repeat, the liquid in my stomach climbing into my throat. "I'm going to be sick again."

CHAPTER SEVENTEEN

FLORENCE

This might turn out to be the greatest mistake of my life.

I've agreed to give Blake the day. One day to prove he had nothing to do with Mae's disappearance. A day to make me sure of it. Against my better judgment, against every cliché trope I know, I don't believe my best friend's husband did this.

I believe he loves her. I believe he wants to find her as desperately as I do.

Which is why, today, while everyone is leaving the ship to explore Costa Maya, we're going to try to seek out Zach and stop him from leaving. Try to find answers we haven't gotten yet. Answers we deserve.

Telling him about the dress is much less risky for Blake than telling Diego. But if, by the end of the day, we haven't gotten any answers or discovered anything that will help us find her, I'm going to tell Diego about the dress, with or without Blake.

Before we reach the shore and everyone begins to disembark, Patton and I eat breakfast on the deck. I mostly pick over my food while watching the woman at the table next to us slather sunscreen on her four children as they wriggle out of her grasp. Next to her, the man I assume is her husband sips a coffee, occasionally looking up to offer her a sympathetic smile but not much else.

It's scorching out today, the sun beating down on me even through my sun hat and caftan. I wave my hand in front of my face, fanning my skin.

"You really should eat," Patton says gently, drawing me back to reality.

"I know." I take a bite of my omelet pointedly. "You slept soundly last night."

He seems to take it as the insult it's meant to be. "I knew you needed your sleep, and I worried if I didn't sleep, I'd end up keeping you awake with my phone calls and emails. I know how the light from my phone bothers you, so I took a sleeping pill and put on my headphones. Are you mad?"

A sleeping pill. Well, that certainly explains how he was able to sleep through so much.

I shake my head, taking another bite. "Nope. Not mad." I guess he meant to be sweet, but in all reality, I can't find the energy to care. As much as I hate to say it, I wish Patton hadn't come on this trip at all. Honestly, I think he feels the same way, though he's too polite to come right out and admit it.

When I look up and see the woman still struggling to put sunscreen on her youngest child while the husband appears completely unaware of her rising stress levels, I drop my fork onto my plate, the metal clattering loudly on the ceramic.

"I don't think this is working."

He pauses, his own fork half lifted to his mouth. "What?"

"This. Whatever this is. I'm sorry. I think you probably agree. Whatever this is...it's not working for me." I wave a hand in the air. "I'm sorry. I know we're sort of stuck together until the end of the cruise, but I'm just going to move my stuff out of the room. You don't have to pretend to care about any of this anymore. You're off the hook."

"I'm not pretending," he says in a defiant whisper. "I care about you, Florence. And it's terrible what's happened to your friend. But I don't know how to be around you right now. I don't know what to say or do. I feel like I'm in the way or saying the wrong thing *one hundred percent* of the time. I'm doing too much or not enough. It's not your problem, and I've tried hard not to make it your problem, but I'm not sure what you want from me. I'm sorry I wasn't better prepared for this." He sighs. "I don't want to break up, for the record, but this timing made sure we didn't stand a chance."

I stare at my hands, twisting the napkin in my fingers. "I just think I need to focus on finding Mae right now and you need to focus on work, and it's not helping either of us to pretend any differently." I swear I see the tension leave his body. I'm doing the right thing, even if it's hard. I didn't expect it to be *so* hard

149

though. I do care about him. Maybe more than I realized.

I stand up, needing to get away from him.

"Where will you go?"

"I'm not sure. Maybe I'll see if I can crash with Blake."

"In the same bed?"

I don't miss the flare of jealousy in his eyes.

"Oh, Jesus. We are so far past that at this point. Neither of us is sleeping anyway."

"What if Mae comes back?" he asks.

I twist my lips, unable to answer, because I think the truth is that none of us expect her to. The realization hurts more than anything else.

"We only have two more nights. I'll figure it out. I can sleep on the floor if I have to. You don't need to worry about it."

He stands, reaching for my arm, but stops himself before he grabs it. "No, wait. That's ridiculous. Just sleep in the room with me. We can be broken up, fine, but you don't need to sleep on the floor when there's a perfectly good bed that we split the cost of."

"I just can't." I turn away, moving across the deck quickly. "Please respect that. I'm sorry."

He doesn't chase after me or make a scene, which I'm grateful for if not a little let down, as I enter through the door and into the dining room. I come to a stop when I nearly run into a familiar face.

"Hi!" I shout, partly startled and partly relieved. "Oh my god! You're Zach!"

"Do I know you?" he asks, his dark brows drawn down. Up close, he's even more attractive than he was that night. A sharp jaw, the shadow of facial hair across his chin and cheeks, blue eyes surrounded by such thick lashes they appear as if they're straight out of a dream.

"I'm..." I lower my voice, trying to tame my trembling hands. "Sorry. I'm Mae's friend. Diego told me he talked to you. He said he told you she was missing."

"Oh." He looks away, startled by the trap he's walked into. "Right." He nods seriously, looking around as if checking to see if anyone's watching us.

"Anyway," I say quickly, hoping he won't try to leave, "Mae always raved about you in college. I can't believe she didn't tell me you were the one she was dancing with Tuesday night."

"Ah!" He snaps his fingers. "Right! *That's* why you look familiar! I couldn't figure it out."

"You also approached me at the bar when we first boarded," I tell him, sidestepping to let an older couple out the door and moving closer toward him. "You asked if she was Mae. I guess you recognized her right away."

"Yeah, I did. She, uh, she's always been able to catch my eye." His smile is nostalgic. His eyes become sad. Ghosts of memories dance behind their glassy exterior. "I couldn't believe she was here when I saw her. I mean, what are the odds, you know? But, even before I asked you, I knew. I'd know her anywhere."

"How long had it been since you saw each other?"

His eyes widen. "Saw each other?" He puffs out a breath of air. "Gosh, five, six years, I guess? It had to be.

We hadn't spoken in...well, at least five years. She stopped coming by my house when they were in town for the summers. I didn't really know why, but I assumed she'd met someone. She told me Tuesday night that she'd gotten married."

"Yeah."

"Any chance he's an asshole?" He laughs. "Sorry. Kidding. But, yeah, it was a shock. I hadn't heard."

"She told me she loved you...back then. You guys were pretty serious, I guess?"

He runs a hand over his mouth. "Yeah, we were. At least, I thought so. I never really saw her marrying anyone else, to be honest." He's quiet for a long while, as I try to decide what to say. Before I can, he says, "My parents own the Shoreline Grill. I'm not sure if you're familiar with it, but it's the little restaurant near the hotel where her family would always stay. Growing up, I was there all the time, playing out in the sand in front of the restaurant, trying and failing to surf when I got old enough." He chuckles. "I don't know if she told you, but that's where we met. We were pretty much inseparable after that first summer. They were only in town for one week every summer, but we spent every bit of it together. When she was sixteen, when her mom got really sick again for a while, she spent the whole summer with my family. It was... That was when I realized I loved her."

He looks over at me as if he'd forgotten I'm here, then clears his throat. "Anyway, then one year, she just...didn't reach out. I called and texted her a bunch of times and never heard back. Or, when I did hear from her, it was a text here or there saying she'd call when she had a chance. She never did. I guess it's when she met her husband." He shrugs, failing to look unfazed. "We loved each other, but the timing was never right. We were just stupid kids, you know? I'm... I'm so sorry to hear she's missing. I'm sure it's just a misunderstanding."

When his voice cracks, I realize I want to believe him. Wholeheartedly.

Am I a fool?

"What happened between the two of you that night? You were dancing and then we left. Did you plan to meet back up at the bar?"

"Yeah. I wanted to talk to her, and I kept trying to, but she said it would be too hard to explain everything to you. I just wanted to catch up, you know? I think we were both just in such shock to be seeing each other after all these years. So, she told me to walk away and act like I was just some random guy. She said she would meet me at the bar at three if I still wanted to talk. To be honest with you, I wasn't sure if she would actually be there or if she was just trying to blow me off again. But when I got there, it was just like old times. We tried to catch up on everything. She told me about her parents and her marriage, about you, and her job at the assisted living facility. I caught her up on my parents and the bachelor life. Once we got going, it was hard to stop. *Talking*, I mean. It was...really good to see her again."

Something in his tone sends warmth creeping up my neck. "Did anything happen between the two of you? After you left?"

He hesitates but eventually shakes his head. "I walked her back to the elevator and kissed her, but she stopped it. She told me she couldn't do that to her husband. So, I did the only thing I could do. I gave her a hug and said goodbye." Tears fill his eyes and he coughs, looking away long enough for them to disappear. "Which is why I ran when I saw her husband in the casino. I recognized him from dinner that first night and assumed he'd heard about the kiss. I didn't feel like dealing with that."

"You ran from Blake?"

"He didn't tell you?"

"No, I don't think so. Honestly, the past twenty-four hours have been such a blur."

"Well, if you see him, apologize for me. It was the wrong thing to do."

"Kissing her? Or running?"

He gives me a sheepish grin and shrugs one shoulder. "Both, I guess. I'm... Look, I'm not a bad guy. Our situation is just complicated. Obviously, I misread it that night. It was my bad." He looks down. "Anyway, she'll turn up. She has to."

I swallow, no longer able to feel the optimism he carries. "Well, I'll let Blake know you're sorry. And thank you for talking to me. For not running away."

"If I'd realized she was missing, I would've talked to him, too. I hate that this is happening. Especially to her parents." He pauses. "How are they handling it?"

"Not well," I admit. "They're on their way down, but

I'm not sure what they'll be able to do. There's not much any of us can do at this point."

"They're sweet people. They were always kind to me. Though I'm sure her dad wanted to kill me a few times."

At the word *kill*, I remember why I'm here. Why I wanted to find Zach in the first place. "Oh! Hey, one more question. When you last saw Mae, was she wearing this dress?" I hold up my phone, showing him the photo I snapped of the dress draped across Blake's bed last night.

"No," he says, hardly looking at it.

"You didn't even look."

"I don't have to," he says quickly. "She wasn't wearing a dress. Not when she met me at the bar."

"She wasn't?"

"No. She was wearing sweatpants and a T-shirt. She'd changed from when we were dancing, said she wanted to be comfortable."

I lock my phone screen. "And what time did you take her to the elevator? Do you remember?"

"I guess it was around four thirty or four forty-five."

"Okay. Great. Thanks."

"No problem," he says, patting my arm. "I really hope you find her. If you guys need anything else, let me give you my number. I know you don't owe me anything, but is there any way you could give me an update when you find her?"

"Of course."

"Thanks." He rattles off his number, and I type it into my phone.

"Got it. Thank you again. I'll let you know when we have news."

"Thanks. It was...well, it was good to officially meet you, though I wish it were under different circumstances." With that, we say goodbye and he walks away as I zip off to update Blake.

CHAPTER EIGHTEEN

BLAKE

When Florence finds me on the upper deck overlooking the water as we near the port, I'm embarrassed to admit I've been thinking of jumping myself.

Not actively planning, mind you. More like...quiet contemplation. What are those things called? When you picture doing something terrible or imagine a horrific accident? When you imagine how much blood would splatter if you walked out in front of that bus, or how it would sound if you just kept the car going straight around that curve? Intrusive thoughts, I believe. Lately, I find myself having them more than ever.

What would happen if I jumped? Would anyone notice? Would they find me in time? Would they try?

I stare out over the water, considering the fact that Mae could very well be underneath the surface right now. Did she go over on purpose? Did someone push her? Will I go to my own grave never knowing?

I imagine her body free-falling over the edge. Would

she have screamed? Called out for me, maybe? Or was it peaceful? If someone forced her over, did they knock her out first, or did she feel every painful minute as her lungs burned for oxygen?

It's too terrible to think about, and yet, I can think of nothing else.

So when I hear someone calling my name, it takes me several seconds to register it and several additional seconds to turn around and see what she wants.

"I talked to him," she says, out of breath and flushed, as if she ran here. Does anything matter enough to run for anymore? "Did you hear me?" she asks when I haven't answered quickly enough. Then again, I can't even remember what she said.

"Huh?"

She snaps her fingers in front of my face. "Blake? Hello? Are you listening? I talked to him. I talked to Zach."

The name brings me back to reality with a searing rage. "You *what?* How did you find him? Where was he? What did you say? What did he say?"

"I ran into him in the dining room and asked him everything. About that night. About them."

Them. The word burns me from the inside out.

"They weren't having an affair, Blake. It was a shock to them that they were both on the same ship. He said they hadn't talked in years. Since she met you. Mae *didn't* leave with him."

"And you believe that?"

The wind whips her hair in her face, and she brushes

it back just as quickly. "Yes, I do. He said they wanted to have some time just to catch up, but she was worried about telling me, so they thought it was better to wait and meet after I went to bed. Nothing happened. He took her to the elevator and said good night."

"So he says." I scoff, rolling my eyes.

"Yes, but there's more."

"Listening."

"He said that when he met her at the bar, she was wearing sweatpants and a T-shirt. Not the dress we found in your room."

Suddenly, I'm hyperaware of everything she's saying. "Wait, what?"

"Yes." She looks relieved to finally have an active participant in this conversation. "She changed clothes before she met him. Which means I was right. She *did* come inside your room and change. She must've pushed the dress under the bed so you wouldn't see it if you woke up before she came back."

"*If* she was planning to come back. But then why wouldn't she take anything else with her?" I picture it: her changing out of her dress next to the bed, occasionally glancing over at me. Did she feel guilty for what she was going to do? Did she think about it at all? What if she'd woken me up? Would she have canceled her plans? Or lied to me about where she was going? "How do we even know he's telling the truth?"

"We don't, but it would be easy enough to prove, wouldn't it? We could ask Diego to look at the footage. To see what she's wearing that night."

"Great. Let's do it."

"Now you think it's a good idea?"

"If she did change before she met him, then I have nothing to worry about. The dress being in the room doesn't make me look more guilty."

"Unless…" She stops.

"Unless what?"

"Nothing. Forget it."

"No, unless what, Florence?"

"It's just something Diego said to me. It's nothing."

"What did he say?"

"He…" She shifts her feet awkwardly, not meeting my eyes. "He sort of hinted that he thought you'd woken up when Mae came back to the room. Maybe it woke you up and you followed her and saw her with Zach."

"And then what?" I don't even have to ask and she doesn't have to answer. "Is that what *you* think happened?"

"No, of course not. I trust you, remember? We're on the same team. Which reminds me, how do you feel about teammates sharing a room?"

"Huh?"

She huffs. "Would it be too big of an issue if I slept in your room tonight?"

My head tilts to the side. "What? Why? Where did that come from?"

"Patton and I broke up. It's not a big deal. I can sleep on the floor or whatever. I just need somewhere to be that isn't around him."

"Yeah, sure," I say, shrugging one shoulder. "Not like I'll be sleeping anyway."

"Thanks."

"But I do think we should ask Diego what she was wearing in that video. We don't have to mention the dress, but I want to know if Zach was lying to us," I tell her.

"Do you think he is?"

"I don't trust him," I say firmly. I also don't want to give up on the idea that Mae might've been in our room more recently than that night, though it now seems unlikely.

"Fine. Yeah, okay. When? We'll have to go back to the room to call him unless he gave you a number to reach him."

"There's a way to message him on the app. It's how I sent him a photo of Mae, but you can't call within it. We need something quicker than that. Let's go back to the room."

"Great." She starts walking. "That'll give me a chance to get my stuff from my room anyway."

"I keep forgetting to ask if you've heard anything else from her parents," I say when we get to our deck.

She runs her hand through her hair, scratching her scalp. "No. Her mom texted once to tell me to keep them updated, but I haven't had a ton of service. I'm probably being terrible. I know how worried they must be. Remind me to call them before we leave the port, okay?"

"Sure."

Florence stops before we pass her room. "Okay, I'm

going to go get my things, and I'll be right there. Go ahead and call Diego without me and let me know what he says."

I don't have to be told twice. I continue on to my room and let the door slam behind me as I reach for the phone and press the security office's extension.

Within seconds, a young man's voice comes across the line. "Security."

"I need to speak to Diego please."

"I can check to see if he's available. Can I tell him who's calling?" I consider giving him a fake name. Will I have annoyed his boss enough that he'll make up an excuse not to take my call? "Sir?"

"Blake Barlowe. Tell him it's urgent."

A few seconds later, Diego's voice comes across the line. "Yes, Mr. Barlowe? Do you have an update for me?"

"More of a question. In the video you have of my wife at the bar, do you recall what she was wearing?"

"Excuse me?"

"Was she wearing a dress?"

He's quiet for a minute. "Um, no. I don't... Hang on. Give me a second." I can hear him typing something, then he says, "No. She's wearing a T-shirt that has something written on it... Vandalay Industries?" He reads the words slowly. "I think that's what it says, anyway. The quality isn't the greatest, as you know."

Her favorite *Seinfeld* shirt. The memory of it sends a pang through my chest.

I don't know how to feel. On one hand, this probably absolves me of suspicion in Florence's eyes, but it means my wife was here, in this room with me, just hours before she disappeared. Did she put on comfortable clothes with the intention of leaving me?

More and more, that's how it feels.

"Why are you asking?" Diego asks.

"We, uh, we found a dress in my room. A dress I thought she was wearing that night. I'm guessing when she used her key card, she must've come back and changed into the T-shirt." As soon as I say it, Florence's warning rings in my ears, and I regret it. Now he's sure to think she woke me up and I followed her. That I saw her with him and did something terrible.

It's what I would think if the situation were reversed.

"I see. Yes, she must have. She's not wearing a dress here."

I change the subject. "Have you heard anything else from the Coast Guard?"

"Unfortunately, there's nothing to report. They've found no evidence to indicate she went into the water. Of course, that doesn't mean anything. It's still an ongoing investigation."

"Right. Okay. Thank you."

"You're welcome, Mr. Barlowe. I should tell you, *advise you*, rather, that when we make it back to shore, the police will be there to question you. They'll want to take an official statement and declare her missing. I can't stop you from leaving today while we're at our port of call, but if you don't, just be prepared for that when we return the day after tomorrow."

Something in his voice almost sounds like he's

encouraging me to get off the ship. Encouraging me to run. That's what a guilty husband would do.

"Understood. I'm not going anywhere," I say. He doesn't know I've already spoken to the police myself, and I don't bother to tell him. With more force than necessary, I end the call.

I use my phone to look up the number for a lawyer. How do I even know what type of lawyer I need at this point? I'm not worried about a criminal lawyer yet, even with Diego's threats. I want someone who can do something about how badly this is all being handled.

I want someone to do something. Period.

I scroll through a few pages of results, and each website I click on takes several minutes to load. So much for onboard Wi-Fi.

When I find a law firm that claims to cover cases against cruise lines for accidents or injuries, as well as criminal law, I make the call.

"Hanson and Janson, Kelsey speaking. Whom do I have the pleasure of speaking with?"

"My name is Blake Barlowe."

"Thank you, Mr. Barlowe. How may I help you?"

I inhale, preparing myself. "Hi. I'm not sure which of your lawyers I need to speak to, but I'm on board a cruise ship ported in Costa Maya right now, and my wife has gone missing."

"Oh no," she says with a gasp. I can hear her writing something down. Her concern is believable. "I'm so sorry to hear that. When did she go missing?"

"Very early yesterday morning. The crew on board

has been completely useless. I've tried to contact the police there, but they say they can't do anything until we return to port. I'm just running out of options. I don't even know if you can help, I just…" I sigh, not sure what to say next.

"Okay, I completely understand, sir. What I can do is pass this message on to one of our attorneys and have them give you a call back. Does that sound okay?"

"When will they be able to call me back? We're in port now, but once we're out on the water, I may not have service."

"I understand. I'll do my best to get them to call you back today. What time do you leave port?"

"Um, hang on." I tear open my suitcase, flipping through the itinerary. "Five o'clock."

"Okay. Both of our attorneys are in court right now, but if they have a chance to return to the office, I'll have someone call you today. If it's not today, Mr. Hanson will be back in the office tomorrow morning. I can have him give you a call then."

"That may not work," I remind her.

"I understand. What time will you arrive at your next port?"

"We'll be back in Tampa Saturday morning at seven." Two days from now. It can't wait. None of this can wait.

She clicks her tongue. "I'll notate that for them as well, and we'll do our best to have someone return your call today. What would be the best number for them to reach you?"

I rattle it off for her.

"Great. Okay, so I've got that, and we'll be in touch just as soon as possible."

I end the call, throwing my phone onto the bed with as much force as I can muster. At this point, I can practically feel the scrapes from yet another brick wall.

CHAPTER NINETEEN

FLORENCE

I'm shoving the last of my things into my suitcase when I hear the magnetic lock on the door whirring, signaling that someone has used their key card.

When it opens, Patton looks just as shocked to see me as I am to see him.

His eyes flick down to my suitcase and his jaw tenses. "Sorry, I didn't know you'd be in here. You're... You're really leaving, then?"

"I said I was."

"Can we talk about it? Can I change your mind?"

"Do you even want to?"

"Of course I do. I don't understand what I've done."

"It's more about what you haven't done, honestly. Crisis always shows one's true colors, and I'm realizing I don't always want to come in second to your job. I don't want to be the one rubbing sunscreen on our children while you sip your coffee and don't notice me struggling."

His eyes narrow, head tilted to the side as he tries to understand the reference. "What was that?"

"Nothing. Just forget it." I try to move past him to grab a pair of shoes I missed, but he blocks my way, a hand held up in the air.

"*Wait!* Look, I know I work a lot, but I thought you liked that. When we first started dating, you told me you were impressed by my work ethic. You said you'd never dated anyone so *grown up.* I'm still that guy. I didn't change, Florence. *You* did. You're changing the rules without giving me a new instruction manual."

"Yes, I know. But everything is different now. I like that you work, yes, but when my best friend goes missing, I guess I just thought you might skip a conference call once or twice."

He waves his hands in the air with exasperation. "So tell me that! You've completely shut me out of all of this. If you want my help, tell me."

"I shouldn't have to tell you!" I shout, then lower my voice, forcing myself to calm down. Reaching past him, I grab the shoes and shove them into my bag. "I'm sorry, I don't have time for this." I turn around, zip my suitcase and drop it to the floor.

"I think you're just using this as an excuse."

I spin back to face him. "What's that supposed to mean?"

"I think, for whatever reason, you've decided you don't actually want to be with me and this is just a convenient excuse for you to dump me."

"Convenient?" I cry. "You think my best friend's disappearance is convenient?"

He lifts a hand in defense. "Bad choice of words. I'm sorry, I'm just..." He lets out a breath. "I really like you, Florence. This has all thrown me off. I'm sorry, I'm not sure how to act or what to do. I've never dealt with this before."

"Funny, neither have I." I start to walk past him, but he touches my arm.

"Can we please just talk about this?" His voice is desperate. Pleading. "Tell me what to do, and I'll do it. Let me get you off the ship. Blake too, if you want. Let's get off and fly home. It'll be safer. Then we can get in touch with the police and try to get some real answers." The thought brings tears to my eyes, which he misreads as me being grateful. "Come on. We can leave right now."

"You don't get it," I say through my tears. "I can't just leave the ship. This is where she was. Leaving now will be like abandoning her."

"How? For all we know, she's not on the ship. For all we know, she's back in Cozumel, and every minute we're here is a minute farther from her."

I shake my head, swiping a finger under each eye. "I can't leave. I just... I can't. And anyway, Blake won't leave either, and I can't abandon him."

"Did you ask him?"

"I don't have to."

He presses his lips together. "Then what can I do? Name it."

I start to turn him down, but then a thought occurs to

me. "Actually, maybe there is something. Can you look into a man named Zach Carter? Like, could your company find more than an internet search could? And fast, too? Like today?"

"Yeah, sure. It shouldn't be a problem. What can you tell me about him? Who is he?"

"He was a friend of Mae's and ended up on this cruise. They... He was the one I told you she danced with Tuesday night. He's supposed to live in Tampa. His parents own a restaurant called Shoreline Grill."

"Yeah, okay. I should be able to find out something. Is there anything specific I should be looking for? Background? Credit?"

"Just anything that might make him dangerous."

His face goes serious like I've just given him a mission he's ready to accept. "You think he had something to do with her disappearance?"

"I don't know, really. He doesn't seem like a bad guy. But he was the last one to see her before she disappeared, so if there's anything shady about him, I want to know."

"Okay. Sure. I'll see what I can find out."

"Thank you." I reach out, squeezing his hand. "Will you just call or text me as soon as you find anything? Especially if it's anything suspicious?"

"Of course."

"Thank you," I say again. I press my lips to his cheek briefly, then hurry from the room.

CHAPTER TWENTY

BLAKE

Florence and I walk along the deck again after she brings her things to my room. Neither of us says it, but I'm fairly certain we're both watching the shoreline—the people bustling about, soaking up the sun without a care in the world—and hoping to see Mae in the crowd.

As if she might just pop up and say sorry and that she'd been in the gift shop all this time.

As if, somehow, this might have all been a misunderstanding.

I find myself begging to wake up from this nightmare. To rewind time and never have gotten on the ship in the first place.

But would that have stopped this? What if she'd always meant to leave me on this vacation? What if the ship only provided an easier way to accomplish that? What have I done that's so wrong?

I just can't make sense of it, and then, when I try, I

feel guilty for giving up on her. That's what this feels like. I'm starting to accept that she left me, and I hate it.

Because if she didn't, I'll never forgive myself for these thoughts, and the truth is, I'll likely never know.

When the sun reaches its peak in the sky, scorching my skin as the midday heat sets in, I add another tally to my mental count of days without Mae. We're up to two, yet it feels like a lifetime. How am I supposed to carry on like this?

I'm going to lose my mind. The waiting, the questions, the not knowing.

I'm not strong enough to play this role.

"We should get lunch," Florence says. "With everyone off the ship, there won't be any lines."

I think she's suggesting it more out of boredom than anything. Or perhaps concern for me. She's been much more concerned about my eating and drinking than her own, though I'm sure she's not doing much better than I am.

I haven't eaten a full meal since Tuesday night's dinner, and yet I don't feel hungry. I don't feel much of anything other than sheer panic at the moment.

We each get a slice of pizza from the buffet and sit at a small bistro table near the window. We eat mostly in silence. I pick at my lukewarm crust, nibbling a bit here and there. I just can't bring myself to do it.

How can I eat when I don't know where Mae is or if she's even okay?

"Oh, look!" Florence cries out, pointing at a seagull as it swoops down to grab a fish in the distance.

I don't mention the way my heart leapt when she said it, how I thought she'd seen Mae. How, for two whole seconds, I'd thought this might all be over. I can't say any of that, though. Not even to her.

I already feel the pressure to turn back to normal. To not make anyone uncomfortable with my grief.

When I don't respond and merely stare out the window, not actually looking at anything at all, we return to our meal. The silence between us should be awkward. We're not used to being alone without Mae as a buffer, but we've no time for awkwardness right now. We're all each other has.

"Last real night here," Florence says softly, more to herself than me. She's right. Tomorrow night, we'll be preparing to leave the ship early the next morning. We should be celebrating. Soaking up our last night in paradise.

I breathe a broken laugh through my nose, though it feels more like a sob. "Somehow, this hasn't been the vacation I pictured when we booked it."

"What are we going to do, Blake?" Her voice cracks as she asks.

"I have no idea," I admit.

"How could we possibly go back to our normal lives the day after tomorrow? Nothing will ever feel normal without her."

My throat is too dry to answer, so I look down at my mostly untouched food. I hear her sniffle, but I refuse to look up. If I see her crying, I'll cry too, and if there's one thing I don't want, it's to be sitting out here crying into my pizza with my wife's best friend.

No, scratch that. If there's one thing I don't want, it's for Mae to be missing. I can handle anything else if it means she comes back to me.

After lunch, I can't bring myself to keep watching for her over the deck railing. It's too painful. Every time I see someone who might be her, only to realize it isn't, I lose her all over again. Florence must feel the same way because when I say I think I'm going to go back to the room and rest, she asks if she can come too.

I don't bother arguing. Again, there's no space for awkwardness in this broken state I'm in. We walk back to the room in silence, though I spy Florence stifling a yawn once or twice. Those are supposed to be contagious, but I don't seem to be catching them. Despite how much I need sleep, my body isn't getting the memo.

I'm worried something is really wrong with me besides the obvious. Like I'm starting to malfunction. To shut down. It would explain why I seem to be rejecting what little food I can get down. Why I haven't had more to drink than a glass of water in two days and it doesn't seem to have affected me. Why all my emotions seem muted lately.

I can't bring myself to care about anything, to feel anything other than overwhelming devastation and hope-lessness.

When I open the door to my room, I know for a fact I can still feel things. I'm not entirely broken. I know this because when I see what's waiting for me in the room, my knees go weak. Fear grips me, then relief. Then confusion.

I freeze. It's definitely not sadness I'm feeling anymore, but I'm not sure it's better.

It takes me several seconds to make sense of what I'm seeing, but when I do, my heart skips a beat as my body turns to ice.

"What the…"

On the freshly made bed, next to a towel-art elephant, is Mae's purse.

She's back.

CHAPTER TWENTY-ONE

FLORENCE

Blake takes off so quickly it startles me. He grabs something off the bed before I see what it is. When he turns around, his eyes are frantic and wild as he searches the room, like he expects someone to be here.

When I realize what he's grasping in both hands, I understand why.

"Is that...?"

"Her purse," he says without looking at me. The small, black clutch has a gold chain and clasp. I'd recognize it anywhere.

"Why is it here?"

It's a dumb question and one he doesn't bother answering.

I try again. "Is *she* here?"

He moves to the bathroom in a hurry, flipping on the light. "She has to be..." he mumbles. "Mae?"

"Are her things in there?"

He unfastens the clasp, checking inside. "Her phone, her wallet, her passport, her key card... It's all here."

"Okay. Okay." I try to think. "How is this possible?"

He picks up the phone on the wall, ignoring me as he jabs his finger into the same button over and over again. I assume he's calling Diego, but soon realize he's calling the steward instead.

When the call goes unanswered, he slams the phone down and darts for the door, swinging it open and hurrying out into the hallway.

"Jacob!" he cries, spotting the steward in the hallway with a bucket of ice in his hands.

The man plasters on a wide smile. "Yes, sir? Everything okay?"

Blake holds the purse in the air. "Why was this in my room? Where did it come from?"

Jacob glances at it, shaking his head with confusion. "I'm afraid I don't know, sir. Is it not yours?"

"It's my wife's, but up until now, it's been missing."

As if he just registered who Blake is, his lips form an O shape and he sucks in a breath. "I didn't... I don't know, sir. Hang on. I'm training today. Hilda cleaned your room. Maybe she found it." He presses his key card to a door and pops his head inside. "Hilda, could you come here for a second?"

An elderly woman walks out, her eyes wide.

"Did you put this on my bed?" Blake demands, holding out the purse.

The woman shakes her head furiously, speaking in broken English. "I no take anything. It all there. *All.*"

Jacob says something to her softly in a language I don't recognize, though I suspect it may be Indonesian, as his nametag has **Indonesia** listed under his name.

She gesticulates wildly as she answers him.

When he turns back to us, it's with a hint of apprehension. "Hilda says she *did* put the bag on your bed, but it was in the guest lost and found. She says someone had tagged it for your room, probably because of the identification inside of it. They would've tried to call you first, then sent it to be delivered for your convenience."

They both study us worriedly.

"How did it end up in the lost and found?" Blake asks.

"I'm sorry, sir. I don't know."

"Well, who found it? Where was it found? Is there some sort of log?"

"No, sir. There are no records. A guest may have turned it in or possibly a crew member. There's no way to tell. I'm so sorry. I realize how frustrating that must be, given your circumstances. Is there...anything missing?"

"Just my wife," Blake says bitterly, turning to walk away.

Back in the room, we go through her things.

"Nothing's missing," he tells me, holding out her phone, wallet, and a tube of ChapStick. "Not even the cash in her wallet."

"Could it have been a crew member who took her? You heard him. Anyone could've turned that in. We should ask Diego to check the security footage of the lost and found."

"Yeah, that's not a bad idea, though it's probably in a *blind spot*." His voice mimics Diego's when he says the words. "Someone here knows something." He holds the power button down on her phone, trying to turn it on, but it's dead. He leans forward and plugs it in, placing her wallet and ChapStick down. Then, he crosses the room and picks up the landline attached to the wall, pressing the button to call Diego.

"I need to speak to Diego please." He pauses. "Yes, it's Blake Barlowe. Tell him it's urgent." Another pause. "Yes. Fine." He taps his finger against the wall, dipping his head down. Seconds later, his head pops up. "Diego, hi. Listen, Mae's purse was brought to our room. Jacob said it was found in the lost and found and returned to us —" He's cut off. "Right, but I wanted to see if you could check the footage for the lost and found. If we had an idea of who turned her purse in, it would help us figure out... Okay. Yep. Thanks."

He places the phone down. "He's going to look into it. I'm not holding my breath."

Did Mae hold her breath when she hit the water? I hate the question as it pops into my mind. Hate that some small part of me has already resigned her to a fate we can't prove.

As he walks back toward me, my phone vibrates.

"It's Patton," I say, reading the screen. "He may have found something about Zach."

"Go ahead," he says, hardly listening.

"Hello?"

"Hey." His voice is firm. Urgent, almost. "I think I found something."

Something inside my chest stirs. "Yeah? What is it?"

"You may want to come see in person. It's...it's not good, Florence."

"Just tell me." I put the phone on speaker and squeeze my eyes shut. "Blake's here, too."

"Okay, before I go on, I have to tell you something." He pauses. "I, um, I lied to you earlier."

The impact it should have on me is softened by the reality we find ourselves in. No lie could compare to how bad our situation is. "What do you mean?"

"When you asked me if I was at the bar with Zach when I was supposed to be in line to board at the Cozumel port."

Blake's eyes go wide and guilt settles in my gut. *He was telling the truth. He really saw them together.* Why didn't I believe him?

"You were there?" Blake demands, looking at me rather than the phone.

"Yeah. To be fair, I didn't *know* it was Zach. I didn't even know who Zach was. I... When we separated, I left Cozumel and came back to the ship instead of going to the café like I originally told you I was going to. I needed to make a call in private, and I couldn't do that there."

"What call? To Zach?" I ask.

"No, to a client. My... My biggest client, frankly. I wasn't trying to make it a big deal. I knew you had a lot going on, but when I was distracted in Cozumel, it was because I was losing him. One of the big guys offered him a deal he couldn't refuse and, when we ported, an email came through telling me the news. I was trying to save the deal, to save my company, if I'm being honest. I know it doesn't compare to Mae being missing, which is why I didn't tell you, but... I was pretty, um, *bummed* is putting it lightly. I needed a drink. Something to help me decompress before I saw you again."

I take in what he's saying, trying to understand it all. "You didn't tell me any of that."

"No, and it's not important right now. I'm only telling you so you understand why I was there. A guy—*this* guy —sat down next to me and ordered a drink. We were both drinking old-fashioneds, so he complimented my drink choice. That was it."

"I'm sorry, Patton. I wish I'd known." Guilt settles in my throat, both for Patton's company and the impatience I had with him, and for not believing Blake.

"I'm sorry I lied. I didn't want to, I just couldn't talk about it yet. I was bitter and angry. I just wanted to go home and try to fix this, but I knew you needed me and... Anyway, it doesn't matter. The point is, I'd honestly forgotten about it until I started looking into him and saw his picture."

"So, you found something?" I ask, choosing to focus on one revelation at a time.

"Well, not exactly. I didn't find anything on Zach, but when I pulled up some of his family history, I saw a red flag. A big one."

"Meaning what?" Blake asks before I have a chance to.

"He has an uncle, Chase, who was arrested several years ago...for human trafficking."

My body goes numb as if I'm suddenly floating above myself. I have no sensation in my hands or feet. My tongue no longer feels as if it's in my mouth.

"What?" Blake's voice quivers, and he clutches his stomach.

"He's in prison. It was low-level stuff, from what I can tell. Most of the charges are from Tennessee, but there are a few from Florida, too. I guess he was going back and forth between them, running operations in both places before he was caught. My question is...did Zach take over for his uncle?"

"No," I whisper, though I don't think either of them hears me. I want to say he wouldn't. That he loved her. I want to say I believed his every word, but then again, maybe Mae did, too.

Maybe we all believe the ones who look nice. The ones who smile at us in just the right way. The ones who wear the nice cologne.

Villains are supposed to be dirty. Creepy. Ugly.

We're supposed to see them, to spot them easily.

But that's never really the case, is it? Most often, the villains are hiding in plain sight.

"What do we do?" I ask, looking at Blake. "We have to do something. Tell someone. We should tell Diego."

"No," Patton says quickly. "No."

"What do you mean *no*?"

"It's not safe. This is serious stuff, Florence. If Zach is involved with the same ring his uncle was, we don't know who else on the ship may be involved as well. If you tell the wrong person, they could take you out. You can't mess with these people."

Blake glances down at the purse in his hands. "He's right. If her purse was found in the staff quarters, one of them could be involved."

"So, who are we supposed to trust? They could *all* be involved. Everyone's a suspect here. The stewards. The kitchen staff. Even the guests. This whole ship."

"We trust each other," Patton says. "It's the only way to be sure we make it back alive."

He doesn't say the quiet part aloud: it's the only way we don't end up like Mae.

PART 3

CHAPTER TWENTY-TWO

MAE

When I come to, my head feels like it's been crushed under a bookcase. It's heavy, sore. I try to look around, to search for Blake, but I see no one. Nothing. The room I'm in is pitch black.

No.

Wait...

Maybe not.

There's something over my face. I tilt my head toward my shoulder, rubbing my cheek against it through the searing pain to confirm—*yes*. Something is over my head. A bag, it feels like.

Claustrophobia sets in immediately as I suck in a breath, the thick fabric pushing into my mouth. It's a rough texture and heavily perfumed in chemicals. My skin is hot and itchy, not to mention terribly raw. I'm tired yet wide awake. My stomach is empty. I can't move my right hand.

Where am I?

Where is Blake?

Florence?

I open my mouth to call out for them, but my throat is too dry. I can't make my voice work.

When I hear footsteps, I freeze. Is it them? Are they coming to find me? Is this a dream?

Thinking back, I struggle to recall my last memory. I remember the cruise... We were supposed to be going on a cruise. Did we ever make it? I can't... I can't seem to remember anything.

Why am I so hungry?

So nauseous?

What is happening to me?

I don't recognize the voices as they get closer to me, nor do I recognize the language that they're speaking. Russian, maybe? Or...German? It's a harsh language. Angry sounding. Then again, maybe they're just angry.

I weigh my options. Should I try to draw attention to myself? Ask them what's happening?

But what if they're the reason I'm here?

My fuzzy mind is beginning to pull things together and as reality sets in, my heart pounds. I'm trapped. Tied up. Something is over my head, preventing me from seeing my surroundings, limiting my airflow.

I gasp for breath as the panic sets in again, but when the voices draw nearer, I somehow summon the resolve to get quiet. I need to understand what's happening. Need to think.

I close my eyes, pressing every point of my body into the surface underneath me. I can sense the water shifting, feel the waves. It's like being in the wave pool at the water park. We're on a boat. The ship. Maybe we made it onto the ship after all.

I run my tongue over my lips, desperate for water. Something to drink. I'm absolutely parched.

Thinking of water makes something tingle in the back of my mind, a hint of a memory. I grasp onto it, clawing and scraping at the corners of my consciousness for where it comes from. Where it belongs.

I was at a bar I don't immediately recognize, with...

Zach?

It's impossible, but something in my gut says it's real. It feels recent.

It comes back to me like pieces of a dream in the early morning—more feelings than images. I was with Zach, I'm sure of it, but where?

He... He left. We said goodbye.

Were we still at the bar? I don't think so, but I can't recall where we were. I remember the smell of him. It made me feel safe. Made me miss him.

Where was Blake?

There was another man. Someone else who came up to me...

I can't picture his face. It's a blur. He handed me something. A jacket. Was it a jacket?

It wasn't mine.

The memory gets fuzzier.

Suddenly, the voices are right next to me. Someone whispers in my ear.

CHAPTER TWENTY-THREE

MAE

The bag is ripped off my head so quickly it's jarring. My neck throbs from the force of it, and I wince. The room is large and dark. Damp. There are a few lights hanging from the ceiling, swaying with the ocean as we move.

A man grabs my arm and pulls me into a sitting position. I'm so sore under his touch, I'm sure this isn't the first time it's happened. What else have I forgotten?

There are four of them. They're unfamiliar to me, their faces marred by the shadows in the room.

"Well, well, well... Look who's awake," the first man says, glaring at me as he clicks his tongue.

"Pretty girl," the second purrs. He's got long, dark hair that hangs down near his shoulders. The first one is a clean-cut blond.

I scoot back farther from them, unsure if I should speak. If I try to start asking questions, I'm scared I won't be able to talk.

A third man bends down next to me and unscrews

the top off a bottle of water. "Drink," he says firmly, his upper lip stiff and unmoving. A heavy accent slurs the word.

I shake my head, trying to refuse, though my throat has practically collapsed from thirst. He grips my chin, squeezing tightly, and dumps the water onto my lips. I hate myself for lapping it up the second I taste it.

Behind him, the rest of the men laugh.

I try to pull back, to catch my breath, but he has a firm grip on me. He doesn't stop pouring, and I start to panic. I suck in a desperate breath and water burns my nose. I sputter. I'm going to drown. I can't breathe. I pull back harder and he jerks away, stepping into line. I gasp, coughing up the water from my lungs. They watch in delight as if I'm a television show meant only for them to enjoy.

The second man steps forward, tracing a finger down the line of dampness on my shirt. His long fingernail scrapes my skin through the fabric. He chuckles. "You need help taking this off?"

I jerk away, but he seems unfazed. The first man swats the back of his head and says something in the language I heard them speaking earlier. Something unspoken goes on between them, but the man doesn't move.

"We're just having fun, aren't we, sweetheart?" the man asks with a wink. He's so close to me I can smell what reeks of soured milk on his breath. He reaches forward, grabbing my breast so hard I cry out.

I fall back, struggling to get away from him, but it's no

use. The men watch it happen but do nothing to stop it. It's only then that I realize my hands are tied behind my back.

I gasp as the bag goes over my head again.

Then my mind goes fuzzy and I'm gone.

CHAPTER TWENTY-FOUR

MAE

When I wake up again, I'm sitting in a chair with the bag already off my head. There's a man sitting across from me, also in a chair. I study the apple in his hand—red. Sweet. Once, I would've turned it down, preferring green. Now, the thought of any food sends my stomach into a frenzy. I've never been so hungry in my life.

He slices into the apple, cutting a huge chunk off and dropping it into his mouth. He chews with an open-mouthed smile on his face.

When he's done, he drags the back of his arm across his lips. "Morning."

I don't bother replying. He stands, dropping the apple onto the ground. I flinch. The thought of it going to waste makes my eyes water. He lifts a foot and stomps down on it, smashing it to bits. Yellow pieces of the apple's innards splatter in every direction.

He walks toward me with a smug grin, still holding the knife. When he nears me, he bends down, using a finger to wipe a bit of apple off the toe of his shoe. He raises it to my mouth. "Want some?"

It's embarrassing to admit how tempting it is to open my mouth, but I don't. More out of spite than disgust. He holds the knife to my chin. "Come on now. Open those pretty lips for me."

My eyes flick to the knife, then move to meet his. The darkness inside his gaze is startling. There's no life there. No humanity.

The tip of the knife presses into my skin, and I open my mouth instantly. He shoves his finger between my lips, running it along my tongue. I taste the salt of his skin, the sweetness of the apple, and something metallic, like the scent on Blake's skin when he's been working outdoors.

After what feels like too long, he pulls his finger out, wiping it dry against my cheek.

"Now then, Mae, don't you feel better?"

My brows furrow. How does he know my name?

He chuckles, seeming to read my mind. "Oh, yes. I know who you are. We all do. You're quite the little celebrity around here. Our guest of honor, so to speak."

"What do you want from me?" My voice is so hoarse it doesn't sound like my own. The only proof it came from me is the sandpaper feeling at the base of my throat.

"*I* don't want anything from you. I'm just the delivery boy."

"We don't have any money," I say softly. "Whatever you think you're going to get, you're wrong."

"Oh, no need to worry about that. He's interested in

something much more"—his gaze rakes over my body—
"*fun* than money."

"*He* who?"

He turns to walk away from me, moving slowly back
to his chair. When he sits down, it's with gusto. He kicks
out a leg, crosses it over the other, and leans back in his
chair with his arms folded over his chest. "Your new
owner."

"My..." I can't finish the sentence. What he's just said
is impossible. And yet, it's not.

"*New. Owner.*" He draws out each word, his tongue
pressing against the inside of his cheek. "That's right.
You, my dear, were sold today. We made a pretty penny
on you, too. You're going to meet him tomorrow, so I'm in
charge of getting you cleaned up today." His upper lip
curls. "No offense, but you reek."

"What are you talking about?" My voice trembles. I
don't want to know the answer.

"Don't worry. I'm sure he'll take great care of you...as
long as you're a good girl." He looks down, laughing
under his breath at his own joke. "You are a good girl,
aren't you?"

My body feels as if it's suddenly liquid. I want to die.
I'd rather die than this. Anything but this.

"It's just the two of us for a while," he whispers.
"What do you say we find out how good you are before
your bath? Trust me, I'm a lot nicer than your new man."

I shudder as he moves toward me with a look I recognize well.

Suddenly, I realize I know him. Memories flash

through my mind. He's the bartender from the ship. The one who served me that last glass of water. The one who brought me the jacket at the elevator after Zach left. The one who followed me onto the elevator. *Benny*.

"You did this," I mutter, piecing it together. "You drugged me. You brought me here."

He doesn't confirm anything, but his smile is confirmation enough. "Come on, honey. I prefer it if you don't talk." He reaches for my face, and I launch myself out of the chair, falling to the floor. I struggle to stand, to make my legs work, but they're like jelly and he's faster. He grabs me and I kick, trying to make contact with anything at all. With a second kick, I do. My foot slams into his ankle, knocking him off balance. He stumbles, reaching for his calf.

"You bitch!" he shouts, red-faced. I kick him again, this time in his knee, and he goes down. When he does, he grabs my leg. I cry out as I feel his teeth dig into my thigh.

BANG.

"What the hell's going on in here?" a man shouts.

Will he save me?

In the distance, a door stands open, filling the room with more light than I've seen in days. If the man who walks in is surprised to find us in this position, he doesn't show it.

The man on top of me releases my leg, turning back to the intruder and barking something at him in the language they all seem to speak. They shout back and forth at each other for several seconds and then the man stands, running a hand through his hair. He waves a hand at me dismissively, as if I'm not worth his time.

"Stay in your filth then, pig." He spits at me, a glob of sticky saliva dropping to the floor in front of me. I scoot back farther. "Won't matter now anyway," he mumbles as he nears the door. "The boss is coming for you."

Chills line my skin. "W-what?"

He turns back, getting the exact reaction from me he was hoping for. With a smirk, he says, "There's been a change in plans. Your purchase was canceled."

"What does that mean? I'm going home?"

"No," he says firmly, staring at me with disgust. "You're not going home. Not your old home, anyway. You're going home with the boss. He... He bought you."

"Wha—" The door opens again, cutting me off. Before I can finish my question, a new group appears. This time, it's three men. I don't recognize a single one of them.

"Sleep tight," one whispers, slipping the bag over my head.

I don't fight it this time. Within seconds, the strong chemical scent fills my nose and I lose consciousness. I welcome the darkness.

PART 4

CHAPTER TWENTY-FIVE

BLAKE

"We have to find him," I say, staring up at Florence over the phone when we end the call with Patton. "We have to find him now." I stand, adrenaline pulsing through my veins. I can't believe she had him and let him go. She spoke to him, and now he knows who she is. He already knew who I was. Our chances of finding him and him not running away are practically zero.

"I have his number," she says, and I spin on my heels.

"What?"

"He gave me his number. I'll call him."

I don't hold out much hope it's the correct number, or if it is that he'll pick up, but I hold my breath as she locates his name in her contacts.

"Hello?"

I huff out a breath as I hear a voice fill the line.

"Zach?" Florence asks.

"Yeah, who is this?" Wherever he is, it's loud. I'm guessing he's off the ship already.

"It's Florence. Mae's friend."

"Oh." He sounds disappointed. "Hey, Florence. Everything good?"

"Actually, we just got some news and I was hoping to update you in person. Can we meet you?"

"Um..." The background noise softens slightly. I assume he's moving away from it. "Yeah, sure. Sure. Where are you at? I can come to you."

"We're still on the ship. Are you off?"

"Oh, yeah. I am. Want to meet me on the little concrete walkway coming into the port?"

I nod enthusiastically as she agrees.

"Cool. See you in a few."

The long pathway from the ship is white concrete and absolutely blinding in the afternoon sun. I squint my eyes, trying to search the crowd for Zach. When I spot him, he's standing by himself, checking his phone.

"Hey," Florence calls loudly, waving a hand over her head.

He looks up, shielding his eyes from the sun despite his dark sunglasses. "Hey." He shoves his phone into his pocket. "So, what happened?"

We exchange a glance as we come to stand in front of him. "We know about your uncle," Florence tells him, brushing my shoulder with hers as she takes a step closer.

"Okay..." He either has no idea what we're talking

about, or he's damn good at pretending he doesn't. "So, this isn't about Mae? I thought—"

"We know he was arrested for sex trafficking."

His smile disappears. "Oh. Yeah. Okay. Why are you telling me that?"

"Because we want to know what happened to Mae."

He blanches. "Hold on, hold on, hold on... You think... I mean, whoa. Wait. He didn't... He's in prison. He didn't have anything to do with Mae."

Neither of us says anything. I once took a course on negotiation, where they taught us if you remain silent for long enough, the other person will just continue to walk themselves into trouble. They'll say more and more until they've said too much. That's exactly what I plan to do with Zach.

He shakes his head. "Unless you're accusing me of somehow being involved with that. But... I mean, I didn't..." He pins Florence with a glare. "I told you everything I know this morning. I don't know where she is. I wish I did. Truly. I hope you find her. I care about her, believe it or not." His eyes cut to me for just a second, but he returns his focus to her.

"You didn't tell me about him," she points out.

"Why would I? Look, I hardly knew my uncle. He's my mom's brother. I met him a few times, but we weren't close. And now he's in prison for something terrible. I don't exactly use it as an icebreaker."

"You're telling us it's just a coincidence?" I demand.

"Yes," he says firmly. "It's *just* a coincidence."

"I don't buy it," Florence says angrily. "How do we

know you didn't help take her? That you haven't picked up where your uncle left off?"

"Because I wouldn't do that!" he says, disgust lining his features. "Look, think what you want, but I told the police all I knew about my uncle back then. I want nothing to do with him."

"Which was what? What did you tell them?" I ask, speaking up for the first time since we arrived.

He turns to face me completely. "I get it, man. I know how you must feel about me. I'd feel the same way. But I didn't hurt Mae. I... I loved her."

"What did you tell the police about your uncle?" I ask again, my words dry.

He groans, looking away. "I didn't know what he was doing, okay? I was just a kid. I'd heard rumors, I guess. Overheard him talking to some of his friends... People I thought were his friends anyway."

"Talking about what?"

His lips press together. "There's this place they all talked about... An island."

"An island? What island?"

"They called it *Isla de los Robados*, which translates to Island of the Stolen. There were rumors of...vodyanoy there." He winces.

"Vodyanoy?" Florence asks the question on my mind before I can.

"It's...they're like mythical sea creatures. It's stupid. When I was a kid, my uncle would tell me stories about vodyanoy, which were creatures that lured women to their death. Like I said, it was ridiculous. But when he came into town, he'd always take a boat out there. My parents would never let me go. They said it wasn't safe."

"And you told the police about the island?" I ask.

"Yes. But they never found anything. I mean, they found the island, obviously, but no women. No sea creatures." He laughs at himself. Then, seeing we're not laughing, his expression sobers. "It's just an island. And, like I said, my uncle is in prison. He couldn't have hurt her. And I certainly wouldn't have."

"If you didn't, someone else could've." It's the first lead I have, and I have to follow it. I have to do something. "Do you remember where the island is?"

"Yeah." He runs his tongue over his bottom lip. "Around about, anyway. It's several hours off the coast. A day's trip from here. Why? You don't think someone took her there?"

My throat goes dry. I don't want to think about it, but I have to know.

"What are you thinking?" Florence asks me.

I meet her eyes. "She wouldn't have left me. I know it. I can feel it in my bones. Do you agree? Do you believe that?"

"You think they have her?" Zach asks. "You think someone is still trafficking people here?"

Ignoring him, I continue to talk to Florence. "I *have* to look for her. It's the first lead we've had this whole time. I can't just pretend not to know about this, and I won't be able to let it go until I know. She's not on the ship. Her things are here. She's not on the ship and she's not in the water and she's not on land. But she's somewhere, Florence. She has to be. You can call me crazy, but I can't give up on her."

"Look," Zach says, "I don't know much about what happened to those girls my uncle took, but I know it happened fast. From what I heard from the police and from overhearing my parents, they didn't stand a chance. If someone here took her, if they took her to the island, she's already gone."

"No," I say firmly, snapping my attention to him. "No. I refuse to believe that. I'm not giving up on her. And if you loved her like you claim you once did, if you care about her at all, you wouldn't either. So, will you help me or not?"

"I will," Florence says. When I look at her, she nods, her voice steady and calm. "I'm in. Whatever you want to do."

"And you?" I look at Zach again.

"I... I mean, I can go with you to the police when we get back, sure. Tell them about the island."

"No. I don't have time to wait."

They both stare at me.

"I have to get to the island now. I have to find her."

"What are you talking about?" Florence asks.

"I'm going to rent a boat. I'm not staying here a second longer."

"Do you have any experience with boats?" Zach asks. "Any idea what you're doing? I can draw you a map, but it's not going to be completely accurate. Even if it is, it's a day's trip from here. You'd only be a few hours ahead of us. Why not just wait?"

"I've been waiting!" I cry. "You just said whatever happens on that island happens fast. We've still got all day here and then all day on the water tomorrow. Nearly two days until we're set to be back at port. And then, it would take another several hours to get the police involved and make it to the island. We're already behind. We may already be too late. I have to go *now*. Will you help me or not? I'm not asking for permission."

He swallows, nodding. "Fine. Yeah. Let me try to make you some sort of map."

I look at Florence while he unlocks his phone. "You don't have to come with me. You should go back, tell her parents what happened. Tell the police. If I haven't made it back, someone should be there to tell people what we know."

"No. I'm coming," she says without hesitation. "You can't do this alone."

"It could be dangerous. Mae will never forgive me if I let something happen to you."

"So then don't." Her smile is small. She understands how serious this is. She understands it may be a fool's errand. That we may be chasing a theory that doesn't pan out. "I'm going with you. No way I'm staying here. You'll need me. You can't do this alone. And, even if you can, I won't let you."

"Fine." I don't have time to argue.

When Zach turns his attention back to us, he nods at Florence. "I just sent you a map I drew on my phone. It's not exactly...good, but it will have to do."

She opens a text, staring at the screen. A few seconds

later, my phone chimes. "Now we both have it in case one of our phones dies."

"Thank you." I study the hand-drawn map, trying to understand what I'm looking at. He wasn't being modest when he said it wasn't good, but I will make it work. Mae's counting on me. I look at Florence. "We should go. We need to find a boat and get started before it gets dark."

We rush down the coast, searching for a boat rental location that's still open. The first two we find don't do rentals after noon, and the next one only has kayaks left to be rented. When we find one that's still open and has boats available, I hand over my credit card and ID while the shop owner goes over the daily rates. I get a discount on his fastest speedboat since the day's mostly over. Stuffing down guilt about stealing a boat from this perfectly nice person, I take my items back and tell him about my experience with boating.

Once he's thoroughly satisfied I know what I'm doing, he hands me a receipt and the key, plus two life jackets, then puts up a sign that reads **Be Right Back / Vuelvo Enseguida** as he leads us down to the water. While he goes over the basics, showing us where everything is and starting the boat, Florence and I put on our life jackets and climb aboard.

Everything is familiar. It's been years since I've done this, but I can handle it.

Or maybe I'm just running on so much adrenaline I can't see how bad of an idea this is. When he's finished and returns to his shop, after wishing us a fun and safe trip and reminding us to return the boat before he closes, I turn to Florence.

"I forgot to ask him where we can get gas around here. Do you mind?"

"Running up there?" she asks. "I'm sure we can find a place."

"I'll feel better if we stop and fill up the gas can before we get too far out. And I don't want to waste any time."

"Okay, sure." She climbs out of the boat, appearing hesitant. "Be right back." While she's gone, I adjust my life jacket and take a seat, fighting to calm my nerves as I watch her jog across the sand. When she's perfectly distracted talking to the shop owner, I grab hold of the steering wheel and ease away from the dock.

She notices as soon as I start moving and realizes what's happening in an instant, but she's too far away. She can't make it to me in time.

That fact doesn't stop her from trying.

At full speed, she rushes across the beach, sand flying behind her. It slows her down significantly, but even at her fastest, she wouldn't stand a chance. I've made up my mind.

"*Wait!* What are you doing?" she shouts at me angrily, arms shoved down to her sides. "*Blake, come back!*"

"I'm sorry. I can't."

"What are you talking about?" She cups her hands

around her mouth, projecting her voice as I get farther away.

"*You have to go back!*" I shout. "You have to go back so you can tell everyone what happened if I don't make it."

"You're an idiot!" Even from where I am, I can see the redness in her cheeks. "Come back here right now! Don't leave me! *Please!*"

Now others are starting to notice us. A small crowd has gathered around her. Thankfully, the shop owner is too busy talking to another group of people to realize what's happening.

"Get back on the ship, Florence," I call to her, turning the boat. "I'm sorry. I'll find her. I'll bring her back."

I don't hear what she shouts at me next over the roar of the engine. Without another word, I speed away.

I'm coming, Mae. Just hold on.

CHAPTER TWENTY-SIX

MAE

I'm aware of voices outside of the room I'm in before I open my eyes.

It takes me a few seconds to come to terms with where I am, with what's happening. Every once in a while, I wake up and still think I'm safe in my bed at home.

But I'm not. Not at home. Not safe. I've been trafficked. You hear about these things, you know? On social media and in the news, but...it's not supposed to happen. Not on vacation. Not to me.

I realize how silly that sounds, but it's the only thing I can think of right now. I don't understand how this happened. How I let it happen.

I'm so angry with myself.

Maybe this is karma. I've always been a firm believer in doing good to get good back. It's why I have dedicated my life to helping others—at the assisted care facility where I work and taking care of my parents, too. I'm not saying I'm perfect by any means, but when something tragic happens, you look for meaning in it. I found meaning in losing my brother. Purpose.

I've spent my life trying to make sure I'm putting into the universe what I want to get out of it. And I've done a pretty commendable job of it, I thought. I've been good, and I got an amazing husband. A perfect best friend. A nice house. A job I love.

It was all going well.

Until the cruise. Until I went against the very core of who I am and allowed myself to be selfish.

Maybe this is the universe punishing me for what I did. When I agreed to meet Zach, I knew what I was walking into. I knew my feelings for him were just as strong as the day I last saw him. I knew—I *know*—I'll always love him. But I love Blake, too. More than anything in this world. I was just swept up in it for a moment. The first man I ever loved walked back into my life, looking at me just the way he always has, and I lost sight of things.

I wanted to feel the way I felt all those summers with him. Wanted to remember a time before responsibilities and stress kicked in. When I look at him, even now, I see the kid he was. The boy building sandcastles with me and burying me in the sand; the preteen who carved our names into the underside of the bar at his parents' restaurant; the teenager who gave me my first kiss, who said he loved me more than anyone had ever loved anyone. The man who told me he'd marry me someday.

It's my fault, not his, that didn't happen.

I met Blake, fell in love, and stopped coming back. Stopped answering his calls. Stopped returning his texts. *I* changed the plan, not him. So, I guess, in a way, I felt I owed him a conversation.

When I saw him across the restaurant the first night, something flipped in me. A selfishness that made me feel both terrible and exhilarated at the same time. Lying to Blake about knowing him was silly. I should've just been honest, but a part of me wanted to keep the secret just for myself.

If I told them who Zach was, I had to share him. To downplay what we were, how much he meant to me once. And the truth is, I didn't know how I felt about him at that moment. I hadn't seen him since I walked away. I needed time to process.

So, for a while, I allowed myself to get swept up in what could've been. In the ghosts of memories of simpler times, in loving him as much now as I ever did. But when he kissed me, I felt the spell break. I knew if I crossed that line with him, there would be no going back. I pictured my husband—the sweet, trusting love of my life—sleeping upstairs in bed, and I knew I couldn't do it. I couldn't take things any further.

Saying goodbye to Zach, knowing it was for real this time, was the hardest thing I think I've ever done. It was the right thing, though. I know that.

Still, karma, maybe? It's small when you compare the two, I think. But maybe not to Blake. Maybe not to Zach, even. I've hurt two amazing men who didn't deserve it.

I force the thoughts away, refusing to wallow in self-pity. No matter what I've done or whom I've hurt, I don't deserve this. No one does.

Whatever is coming for me, whoever is coming for me, I don't deserve this.

My parents don't deserve this.

Blake and Florence don't.

Bitter tears sting my eyes as I hear a door open and shut from across the room I'm in. For a moment, there is only silence. Then I hear slow footsteps heading in my direction.

Click.

Click.

Click.

Click.

Click.

Click.

They stop directly in front of me. I can hear him breathing, smell a hint of the smoky scent of his cologne. I hold my breath.

"Hello, Mae."

His voice is familiar. I can't explain it. Can't put a finger on why, but I could swear I've heard it before.

"Hello," I say softly.

"How are you?"

"I've been better."

He chuckles. "Yes, well, my men do tend to be a little rough. I'm sorry about that."

"What are you going to do to me?" My worst fear comes out in the form of a question.

"I'm going to take the bag off your head." Without

another word, the dark cover is pulled over my face and the room comes into focus. The man has his back turned away from me as he places the bag on the chair behind him.

"They said..." I straighten my shoulders. As much as I hate it, I need to behave. I need to do what it takes to stay alive. "They said you're the boss."

He turns back to face me, and I take in his features. They're softer, somehow, than I expected. He has windswept brown hair and a rigid jaw. His nose looks as if it's been broken before and healed crooked.

When he smiles at me, I notice a scar just under his bottom lip.

"Now then, there you are."

I study him, trying to decide why he sounds so familiar when I've definitely never met him. "Have you... been on this boat the whole time?" Perhaps he's one of the men I've heard outside my door over the past few days. Has it been days? My perception of time is so muddled now.

"No. I just arrived."

I nod. "So, are you? The boss, I mean?"

"I am," he confirms. "Why do you ask?"

"Just curious. Where are we headed?"

He looks down, folding his hands behind his back. When he speaks, he displays a slight accent that wasn't there before. "Isla de los Robados."

"Where is that?"

"Not far."

"What will...happen there?"

Again, his chin touches his chest. "I'm going to let you go."

I take a sharp breath, sure I must've heard him incorrectly. "You're...what?"

"You didn't mishear, Mae. Once we get on the island, I'm putting you on a boat. My crew will take you anywhere in the world you'd like to go. We'll get you set up with a new identity. You'll be free."

I stare at him in utter disbelief. "What are you talking about? *No.* I want to go home. To my family."

"Your family..." He scoffs.

"Yes," I say adamantly. "My family. My husband. My parents. My friends. They will be missing me. I can't just go live a new life. Why would I want to, even if I could? I have no money, no idea where to even start—"

"We can help with that."

"Then why can't you just let me go? Why can't you take me back to Florida? I swear I won't ever tell anyone what happened to me. I won't! You can trust me."

"Take you back? To your family, right?" he asks as if he's egging me on at this point.

"Why do you say it like that? Yes, to my family."

"Because your family doesn't care about you, Mae. Don't you get that? You can't go back to them."

"What are you talking about? Of course they—"

"They're the reason you're here," he blurts out over me.

I open my mouth to respond but find myself lacking in words. "W-what? That's crazy. Why would you say that?"

"Crazy, maybe. But true."

"No. You can't believe that—"

"I don't just believe it. I know it."

"My family wouldn't—"

"They did. *He* did."

"He who? Who are you talking about?" My heart flutters in my chest, so powerless it feels like it might be giving out. "Not Blake. He wouldn't. He loves me."

"Not Blake," he confirms, his deep voice bitter.

"Then who?"

He rolls his fist into one hand, looking away from me. "Your father, Mae. Your father is the reason you're here."

The ground shifts underneath me, the air sucked from my lungs as if I'm in a wind tunnel. "No..." I whisper breathlessly. "Is this a joke? A prank? Don't be cruel. My father would never—"

"He would," he says simply, leaving no room for argument. "He has. He did."

"How can you know that?"

"Because he did the same thing to me."

I swallow, still not understanding. "What are you talking about?"

The man's face softens, and I catch something familiar in his eyes. When he speaks again, I somehow know what he's going to say just before he says it. Even though it's impossible. Even though it can't be true.

"It's..." He looks as nervous as I feel. "It's me, Mae. It's me. Danny."

I blink at him, my heart pounding so loudly in my head I can't hear my own thoughts. What a cruel prank this is. How does he know about Danny? How could he possibly...

"Danny is dead." My voice is cold. Empty. It hurts as much today to say those words as it ever has.

"No." He steps forward. "I'm very much alive."

"You're not Danny."

Lowering down in front of me, he reaches for my arm. He turns it over, baring the pale underside of my forearm, and traces a finger across it gently. Finally, he stops, tapping one spot in particular. When my eyes fall to the white scar near my wrist, a memory floods my mind.

"Do you know what happened here?" he asks gently. "Has anyone ever told you?"

I nod without volition. "Yes, I—"

His smile is soft. "Let me tell you what I remember. It was the Fourth of July. Mom and Dad picked out sparklers for us. I was trying to show you how you could draw things in the air with them, but you were so excited, you kept trying to do it and you dropped yours right on your arm." His eyes go dull. "They blamed me for distracting you."

I cover my lips with my free hand as he turns my arm back over, placing it on my lap. "But...how? I don't understand. You... You died. I was there. I was there when you died, Danny. I watched you drown."

He laughs dryly. "Is that what he convinced you?"

"*Convinced me?* I remember! There was a boating accident. Some dumb teenagers were drunk. They ran into us and you fell out of the boat. I saw it happen! You slipped out of your life jacket before Dad could get to you, and they sped off. I remember everything about that day!"

"You don't. You were two years old, Mae. Whatever memory you have of that day is one they've convinced you is real. I assure you, I am Danny. I am your brother and I'm very much alive."

"I don't understand..."

"I know. I'm going to explain everything to you, but I need to know if you believe me."

Cool tears sting my eyes. "I... I remembered you. When I heard your voice... It's impossible, it would've changed, but there's something about it."

He touches my thigh gently. "I never forgot you."

"But how?" I clear my throat, brushing away my tears. "Were you kidnapped? Why would Dad lie to me?"

"What do you actually remember about the day I disappeared? Talk me through it."

"We went out on the boat."

"Who?"

I try to remember. "Mom wasn't with us, right? I've heard them talk about it enough... She'd stayed back at the hotel because she wasn't feeling well."

He swallows, running a hand over his mouth. "Yeah. It was... It was the year after they discovered she was sick. You're too young to remember that year, but I was eight at the time, so most of it's clearer for me. Dad had lost his job a few months before she got her diagnosis, so we lost our health insurance. When they found out how sick she was and what the treatments were going to cost, I remember how quickly everything changed. It wasn't always bad, you know? They were so in love, like the real deal. Always kissing and touching, laughing, just because. They were the parents who would dance in the kitchen and just...just want to be with each other all the time. They'd hold hands in the car, and he'd sing to her. I don't think either of them could picture their life without each other."

"They're still like that," I tell him. "It hasn't changed. They're so perfectly in love."

He looks down at his hands. "After we lost the house, we moved in with Aunt Deb for a while, but she only had the one extra bedroom, so it was a tight squeeze. Then, I remember one summer, Dad just said, 'We're going on vacation.' It made no sense. We were completely broke, but as a kid, none of that mattered, you know? I just knew that we were going to the beach for the first time, and I was finally going to have something to talk about when I went back to school from summer break."

"I remember the beach that year. I swear I remember playing with you."

"It was the first week that felt normal in so long. Mom even seemed to be getting better somehow," he says. "It was like everything was changing, finally. Then, on our last day, Dad rented a boat and took us out on the water. He was...quiet. Quieter than he'd been all week. At some point, you fell asleep and Dad let me drive the boat." His smile shrinks, then fades completely. "I remember there was this one point when...when I looked up and I noticed he was crying."

"Crying?" It's the last thing I expected him to say.

"He stopped the boat and sat down in front of me and... He hugged me. He hugged me so tight it almost hurt. It was the biggest hug I think I'd ever gotten from him, and he said... He told me Mom was going to die."

I can't stop myself from the sharp intake of breath. "What?"

"He said she was going to die if she didn't have a procedure done, but we couldn't afford it. He said he'd maxed out all the credit cards and the bank wouldn't give him a loan. Her doctors wouldn't do it for her unless we paid for it up front."

Over the years, I've spent an incredible amount of time angry with our country's healthcare system, but every time I hear a horror story like this or watch my family suffer through yet another month of insurmountable medical bills, I'm reminded of just how messed up it is.

"He said..." He looks down, clearing his throat. "He said if I wanted her to live, I had to be really brave. That I needed to *be a man* and protect her because I was the only one who could."

The back of my throat burns with the threat of a sob at his words. "No..."

"He told me a group of men were going to come take me. That I was going to go and live with them. He said it would be easier on me because I was older and I was a boy. He told me if I wanted to, I could say no. And then he'd ask you. If we both said no, it would mean Mom would die."

I shake my head, wanting to argue. Wanting to tell him the father I know would never do that. That the father I know cut my grapes in half until I was seven years old so I wouldn't choke and was the chaperone at all my school dances. But I can't speak. I can't say anything at all. I can only listen to the devastating story unfolding before me.

"He said if I was really brave, if I just went with them, they were going to help Mom get all the help she needed."

"You said yes?"

"I said yes."

"Danny..." I can't speak, can hardly breathe.

"The men came. They crashed into the boat enough to bang it up some—guess I know why now—and I got on the boat with them. You never even woke up, Mae. Dad waved goodbye to me, and I never saw any of you ever again."

"Danny... I... What do you even say to that? I'm so sorry," I whisper. "I'm... God, I'm so sorry. I'm sorry you felt like you needed to protect me. And protect Mom. You were just a kid. How could he do that? How could he..." Anger swells in my chest. "He must've felt so desperate, but that was never the way. If Mom knew, she would never, *never* have been okay with it. She would never have let you... Oh, Danny, do you even know how much she grieved you? How much we all did? Even Dad?

Things were never okay with you gone. It didn't have to be this way."

I feel as if I've been split open, replaying every moment of their grief throughout my life, analyzing every memory, every interaction. How could he carry something so heavy with him all those years? How could he have done something so terrible? How can the man I love be the monster who did this? "We grieve for you every day," I tell him. "I know it doesn't make it okay, but it's the truth. I never thought I'd see you again." I burst into sobs, unable to hold back any longer.

"For years, I used to dream of hearing that, but at the end of the day, none of it matters. It's not your fault. Or Mom's. It was him. He made his choice. We all did. And, if that were it, it would've been bad enough. But this week, when you were meant to be here for a vacation, I heard he called an old friend, someone who helped arrange for me to be taken back then, and told them he had someone new. He told them you were only seventeen, by the way. He gets more money the younger they are."

My stomach roils. "He wouldn't do that."

"He did. We were originally supposed to be picking you up from a bar bathroom, but plans changed and he called us, desperately needing us to get someone on your cruise ship. He forwarded us an email from your friend with the cruise information. Luckily, we have a few of our crew members staffing the local cruise ships, so it was an easy swap to make. Cruises are easy anyway. They drug a drink, get someone off the boat at a port, and from there, it's a cakewalk to get you wherever we need you."

"Hang on." Something about what he's saying forces me to pause. "*Your* crew? You're the boss? I knew that, but... *You're the boss?* How is that possible?"

"The man who bought me used to run the ring. He trained me as bait. No one can resist a lost kid." He sneers. "I was the closest thing he had to a son, and when he was old enough, he passed it all down to me. The whole empire."

"But...why? If you have all the power, why wouldn't you stop this? Why wouldn't you go to the police? How can you be okay with any of this?"

"I have nothing to go back to, Mae. My own family put me into this life. Dad couldn't live without Mom. Period. We were dispensable to him if it meant saving her. These people were more a family to me than you guys ever were. I'm sorry, but I have no desire to stop what I'm doing. I'm good at it. I have respect here. I'm taken care of."

Good at it. The statement rolls over me slowly as I struggle to process everything I'm being told. How can he possibly believe that? How can he care about having respect if this is what it takes to get it? I know... *I know* I shouldn't expect him to be rational. I know I can't begin to fathom the things he's been through, the things he's seen over the years, but still... I can't make myself accept that this person standing in front of me saying such monstrous things can be the same person I've spent my life mourning. The brother I've held on a pedestal all my life. The boy I've wanted to make proud, to do right by. The boy I planned to name my first child after. How is any of this real? How can he be here? How can he do this?

How can he believe any of this is okay?

Because if he believes it's okay, there must be nothing good left in him. No parts of the boy who used to draw sunsets with chalk on our sidewalk, no parts of the boy who watched Saturday morning cartoons with me and loved the kind of gum that you could use to tattoo your tongue. That's the boy I remember.

But, if he's so bad, so evil that he could live with this version of himself, this version of reality... "Then why save me?" I demand. "Why tell me any of this?"

He looks away, appearing almost annoyed with his answer. "Because I couldn't let them take you. Once I heard about this deal, I had to stop it, but I couldn't tell them not to take you. If you were tipped off, or if you went back home, Dad would just try again. This was the only way I could save you. So, now you see why you can't go home. Not ever. It's not safe. He has to believe you're gone for good. That his plan worked."

It doesn't make sense. Dad has never been anything but perfect to me. Loving. Supportive. We talk daily. He's one of the four people I'm closest to in the world. How could he do this to me? How could he just give me away? Never see me again? Hand me off to these monsters? He was the one who interrogated my dates as a teen, and now he was willing to give me away? For God knows what to happen to me? How could he be okay with that?

I clutch my stomach, not sure what part of me hurts more.

"Mom's sick again..." I whisper in answer to my own questions. "Even with insurance, there's a lot that isn't covered."

"And there always will be. At least this way, you're safe."

I look up at him, my tears making his face a blurred mosaic of colors and shapes. "You protected me when they wouldn't."

"You're my sister, Mae. I protected you back then, and I'll protect you always. Any chance I get."

I lean forward, begging him. "Come back with me. Please, Danny. I need you. We can tell the police everything. We can stop this. Together."

"No," he says, looking away. "No, I told you. I'm not going back."

"Because you said there's nothing to go back to, but there is. Me. *I'm* here. I will *be* here."

He puts his hands to his temples, shaking his head. "You're not going back either. Aren't you hearing me? I won't let you. I didn't go through all of this just to send you back out there. Just for him to send someone else after you. Someone I can't protect you from. A ring I can't intervene in."

"Then you're no better than he is!" I cry, stomping my foot on the concrete floor. "You're holding me prisoner, too. I have to go back. I have a husband. A best friend. They need me."

"It's final, Mae." He waves both hands out to his sides

like an umpire calling *safe*. "You may not like it, but I am the boss here. If you don't pick a place, I'll drop you off somewhere by yourself. But you aren't going home. I didn't risk all of this to put you right back with that monster."

"I won't let you do this."

"I'm not asking permission," he snaps. My jaw drops open, but I can find no words or will to argue. I drop my head, refusing to look at him. After a few moments, he turns and storms out of the room, leaving me alone to process my entire world imploding.

CHAPTER TWENTY-SEVEN

BLAKE

As the sun sets on the horizon, thunder rumbles overhead, and I begin to second-guess my decision.

With each passing hour, I realize what a mistake this might've been. Not only am I doing exactly what Diego seems to want me to do by running and making myself look guiltier than I already do, but I also have no true idea where I'm going or if this island even exists. For all I know, Zach made it all up. And, despite my plot to trick Florence earlier, I have an empty gas can and no plans for where to stop for gas or supplies should I need them.

Soon enough, someone will report this boat as stolen, if they haven't already, and then I'll be arrested, both for stealing this boat—which I *did* do—and murdering my wife—which I will go to my grave swearing I didn't. And, to top it all off, I appear to be heading directly into a storm.

I want to think I'll be okay, that I can be smart about this and navigate around the storm somehow, but as the rain begins to pour, I know I'm completely and utterly fucked.

My phone battery is on thirteen percent, and I haven't had service in hours. I slow the boat down as the waves become rocky. I could go off course slightly to try to avoid the storm, but will I end up lost?

The map I have isn't exactly to scale, but even if it was, I'm not used to reading maps that aren't voiced by robots giving me specific, spoken directions. If I get lost and my phone dies while I'm off course, there's no telling where I'll end up.

Another wave hits the boat, and I grab hold of the wheel to keep myself inside the vessel. When I've regained my footing, I tighten my life jacket.

I'll be okay. I just have to go slow.

Slow and steady...

Mae is counting on me.

It's as I'm contemplating all of this and settling nicely into full-blown panic mode that I see a boat in the distance, way off on the horizon.

Boat is an understatement. An insult.

This is a yacht.

A large, white vessel in the distance, though I can't make out much else.

Lightning strikes above it, brightening the evening sky.

It's off course, I think, but honestly, who knows at this point? It's also the only boat I've passed on this trip so far, and I feel in my gut that she's there.

My intuition screams that this is it. That I've found her.

I need to get to that boat.

I turn the wheel, veering sharply to the right just as another wave slams into the boat. Torrential rain begins pelting me, making it impossible to see more than a few feet in front of me or hear anything but my own terrified thoughts.

I can't think straight and certainly can't keep the boat straight.

I focus my eyes on the yacht in the distance, trying to decide which way it's headed. From here, it's hard to tell. I just have to keep moving.

Mae is right there.

So close I can almost see her. I'll have her in my arms in no time.

I can do thi—

A wave smacks into the boat, but I'm not ready. I slide, losing my footing, and my body slams to the ground. I cry out. Another wave splashes in, drenching me and knocking the wind out of my lungs. I fight to stand, fight to catch my breath as the rain picks up. The sound is deafening.

Thunder rumbles overhead.

Angels bowling, my mom used to call it.

I make it onto my knees, trying to grab hold of anything I can reach, as I spy a big wave coming. I can't make it to the steering wheel. There's no time.

No, I have to try.

I stand and lunge just as the wave connects with the

boat. I feel it going up, feel myself losing my footing again. The momentum steals my breath.

I hit the water with my eyes closed, bracing for impact.

I am everywhere and nowhere all at once, in pieces and whole.

Everything hurts.

My head throbs.

My lungs scream.

My hands reach.

But there is nothing.

Nothing there.

No one there.

I am alone.

The darkness haunts me.

CHAPTER TWENTY-EIGHT

MAE

I'm awakened by a commotion outside the door. When I open my eyes, I realize I've been asleep on the concrete floor, though I don't remember moving from the chair.

My head throbs. What is happening?

Danny.

Dad.

The memories come back to me like brutal punches to the gut. I'm so tired. I'm not sure how I'll stay awake through whatever comes next.

When the door swings open, Danny stands in front of me, a confirmation that he is real. That everything he told me actually happened. That it wasn't just a terrible dream. A terrible reality is more like it. "We're here."

"Here?" I croak, my throat dry.

"The island. Come on. We don't have much time. There's a storm headed this way. I need to get you on your new boat and on the way out of here before it strikes." He walks toward me, holding out a hand.

"What? No, I told you, I'm not going."

"Yes, and *I* told *you* it's not a discussion. You *are* going, and that's final."

"I'm not."

"You are."

"Then you may as well let them take me. Because if you let me go, I'm going home. First chance I get, I will find a way home. I'm not running, Danny. I won't."

"It's not smart for you to tell me that," he says.

I cock my head to the side, studying him. Despite the terrible things he's said to me, despite how much easier it may be to lie and figure out a new plan when he leaves me stranded in a new country completely alone, I can't. I don't see anything hard behind his exterior. Something about him softens when he meets my eyes. "I don't think you'll hurt me. Believe it or not, I remember who you used to be."

"That little boy you remember is long gone."

I cross my arms. "That little boy saved my life. Then and now."

He huffs. "Exactly. I saved your life, and this is how you thank me? By making *my* life more difficult? By putting yourself in more danger?"

"I didn't ask you to save my life. Not then and not now. I'm grateful you did, but I don't owe you. I owe the women you're taking. The girls like me. The boys like you. I owe it to my husband to go home to him. To make things I might've really messed up right again. I owe it to Mom to tell her the truth about Dad. About you. I owe it to my best friend to—"

"*Alright,*" he bellows, looking angrier with himself than with me. He curses under his breath, looking away. "I get it. Fine. I'll let the crew take you home. Is that what you really want? Go home, Mae. Walk right back into his trap. But you won't stop what I'm doing. This ring is like a roach. You can cut off its head, but it'll still keep going. Bring me down, bring us all down, but a new version of this will just pop up. You can't escape it."

I study him. Is that really what he believes? He's put up a wall between us again, something not quite hard but not so soft anymore. He's angry. Bitter. But not at me. Somehow, I know this. Just like I know this is the beginning of our goodbye. As if to prove it, he takes half a step back from me, refusing to look my way. "Is that what they told you? That this can't be stopped? That no one can stop what's happening? Is that why you're still here?"

"I'm here because they were right."

"Maybe, but then again, maybe they just need people to believe that so they don't even try." I stand up, drawing his attention to me and moving forward so we're nose to nose, practically the same height. "I'm going home to make things right. Starting with Dad. I'm not going to let him get away with this."

He looks away again, shaking his head. A muscle in his jaw tightens. "It's your funeral. If that's what you want, you can go. I won't stop you. But, for the record, I think it's a terrible decision."

"Well, for the record, I think you staying here is a terrible decision. So, I guess we're even." I look down, anger dissipating, then glance back up with a small smile. "Danny?"

His eyes meet mine without a word.

"Thank you," I whisper, pressing up on my toes to wrap him in a hug.

He's tense in my arms at first, obviously uncomfortable, but eventually, I feel him relax. His arms go around me cautiously. "I should've known. You always were stubborn. Even back then."

I squeeze him tighter, then let go, dropping back down. "I don't want to lose you. I just got you back."

He shrugs one shoulder. "I'll always be around."

"Not really. Not in a way that counts."

He sighs. "Mae, don't do this."

"Do what?"

"I'm glad you've lived a life that's been easy, but most of us—"

"*Easy?*" I shout, slapping him in the chest. He doesn't flinch. "I lost my brother when I was a toddler. My mother has been dying my whole life. I may not have had the life you have, but nothing about my life has been easy!"

He pulls me into another hug, and tears stream down my cheeks without warning. "I love you, too, baby sister. And I always will. Now, let's go."

Without saying any actual goodbyes, he leads me to the upper deck of the cargo ship we're on and speaks to a group of men I don't recognize in a language I can't understand. The island we're on is small and rocky, ominous. A thick fog has begun to settle in, making the dreary island that much more chilling. I don't like the feeling it gives me.

Minutes later, I'm taken off of one boat onto the bleak island and then shown to a smaller boat.

Danny follows close behind us, but when we near the boat, he slows his stride. As the men pass by us, he doesn't touch me, hardly looks at me in front of them. When they board, hauling supplies and untying ropes, it gives us a moment of privacy. He speaks to me while staring at the horizon, his eyes squinting in the sun. I try to memorize them. Remember the way he looks, the way he sounds. I never want to forget. "They will get you back to shore safely, okay? They'll take care of you. Keep you safe. What you do once you're back home is up to you. Just promise me you'll take care of yourself."

"I will. But promise me something too, okay?" I say, keeping my voice low. "Promise me that you know there will always be a place for you should you decide to come home."

He nods once, stepping back and gesturing forward as I cross the sandy shore toward the boat. I try not to cry as we pull away from the shore. He waves with a hand over his head. For a moment, he looks nothing like a man in charge of a criminal empire and everything like the little boy I remember.

On the way, I sit quietly, the wind whipping in my face. We pass through the tail end of the storm and I wrap my arms around myself as rain soaks my clothing, but it's over almost as quickly as it started. Further into the night, once it's completely dark out and we're surrounded by an empty sort of nothingness, I watch in awe as we pass a yacht on the water.

Passing it makes me think of the vacation I was meant to take, the cruise I'd been dreading. Now, all I want to do is start over. Take an actual vacation with the man I love and my best friend. All I want to do is kiss my husband.

The wind picks up and I wrap my arms around myself, wondering how it cooled down so fast. I think of what I'm going to say to everyone when I get back, how I'm going to explain what happened.

How I'm going to confront my father.

How I'll brace my mother for such devastation.

When I'm not worrying or planning, I sleep. The few times I am awake during the trip, the men provide me with bottled water and prepackaged snacks, but it does nothing for the hunger I feel. My stomach is in a constant state of agonizing cramps, begging for something with sustenance. When we finally get back to the port I departed from not so long ago, a full day has passed and we're creeping into a new evening. I'm sunburned and exhausted.

As we get closer and closer to the dock, I stand. My heart could explode from how excited I am to be home. To be safe.

I jump out of the boat when the water is still waist deep and bolt for the beach. My lungs and legs burn, but it's not enough to stop moving. Nothing could ever be enough at this point.

On dry land, I go to the first place I can think of. Shoreline Grill hasn't changed a bit since I last saw it. I walk across the sandy patio and past the metal high-top tables and the chalkboard easel displaying today's special. Approaching the counter, I lean over it and draw the attention of a young waitress.

"Hi, do you think I could use the phone?"

"Um..." She hesitates. "Let me check." She turns and disappears into the kitchen. A few seconds later, she returns with an older woman who looks at me dubiously.

"How can I help you, hon?"

Zach's parents must've hired someone to run the restaurant for them, as her name tag says she's the manager. For as long as I can remember, they were the only ones running this place.

"Sorry. I've had a bit of an emergency, and I lost my cell phone. I was just hoping to use the landline really quickly if it's not too much trouble. I know the owners if that helps."

She looks at the girl, then back at me. "Yeah, sure. Fine. But don't stay on too long. We have to take to-go orders." She lifts the corded phone from underneath the counter and passes it to me.

"Thank you. I promise I'll be quick." Florence and my parents are the only people whose numbers I know by heart, and calling my parents isn't an option right now, so I call Florence. As it rings, I realize she may still be on the ship, as I have no way of knowing what day it is. Nights bled into days while I was being held captive, and with no window to see the sun rising and setting, I'm not sure how long I was down there.

"Excuse me, could you tell me what day it is?"

The woman, who's scrubbing the curiously clean bar a few feet away from me, chuckles. "You sound like me, honey." She glances down at her watch. "It's Friday night."

Friday. The boat isn't set to arrive until Saturday morning at seven, which means she's in the middle of the ocean somewhere without phone service. When it goes to her voice mail, I leave her a quick one.

"Hey, uh"—I lick my parched lips, my throat too dry —"it's me. Mae. Look, I've got a lot to tell you and I'm sure you guys are worried sick, but I'm okay. I'm safe. I'm back in Tampa and I'm using someone else's phone to call you now because mine...I'm not even sure where mine is. Some guy took it when he took me, and... I'll explain it when I see you, okay? Will you just tell Blake that I'm okay? And that I miss you guys? I'll be waiting for you when you get back, okay? Seven sharp. I love you, Flo. Okay, see you soon."

When I end the call, the woman is still working on the same spot on the bar with her rag. "Thanks again."

"You're welcome, honey. I hope you find your friend and get the help you need." She moves toward me, lifting the phone and putting it back in place. "You aren't alone, okay? Addiction is a disease."

I nod slowly, realizing why she's come to this conclusion. "Yeah, thanks."

"You hungry?"

"I don't have any money," I tell her. "But thanks anyway."

"Sit." She pats the counter. "I'll get them to whip you something up."

"You don't have to... I'm not an addict. I just..." I pause, unsure how to tell her what I am. What happened to me. How am I possibly going to put it into words, even tomorrow for Florence, Blake, and the police?

"I know, hon. You don't have to explain. I got two kids who struggle. I can only hope someone would do this for them." She disappears into the kitchen, and I scoot up onto one of the stools in front of the bar.

A few minutes later, she returns with a burger and fries. My stomach rejoices.

The next morning, I wake up with my body warmer and more comfortable than it's been in days. The sand isn't exactly my memory foam mattress, but it was a world better than the concrete floor that's been my bed lately.

The sun has just risen in the sky, and I sit up, watching the locals moving past in their sun-protective gear for their daily walks on the beach. As a kid, the idea of living at the beach both fascinated and terrified me. Now, there's something so peaceful about this part of their routine.

I shield my eyes, looking around.

Shoot.

A cruise ship is docked in the distance. It must be close to seven. Have I missed them? Will they have gotten my voice mail? I push myself to my feet, my body heavy and sluggish from sleep. I jog across the sand as quickly as my legs will carry me, pushing forward on my way to them.

Please still be here.

Please.

Please.

I make it in time to see cruisers leaving the ship and heading into security. I search the crowd for familiar faces as I can't be sure this is our ship. My memory of what it looked like is still fuzzy. Hurrying, I jog around to the exit, watching as people leave, looking varying degrees of sad, tired, hungover, and sunburned.

I stand there, jumping a bit every time the doors open and someone appears, only to be let down when, time and time again, it isn't them.

Until it is.

When the doors open and I catch sight of Florence, she's staring at me in disbelief. She glances down at her phone, then back up at me, and instantly drops her bags. Her eyes fill with tears that must match my own as she runs toward me.

"I stink," I tell her before she reaches me. "I need a shower and—"

She cuts off my words by pulling me into a hug I so desperately need. When we connect, she inhales a shaky breath. "I thought I'd never see you again."

I hug her tighter, my body trembling with sobs. At this point, I'm convinced she's the one keeping me standing. "I'm so sorry."

"We looked everywhere for you," she tells me.

"We've been a mess. I just..." She pulls back, rubbing a hand over my cheek. "I can't believe this is real. Can't believe you're here."

"I'm real." I look over her shoulder, searching for the one face I so desperately need to see. "Where is he? Where's Blake?"

When I meet her eyes again, there's a new sort of sadness in them. "He... He got off the boat, Mae. When we couldn't find you, he was convinced you'd been taken and he couldn't wait. He rented a boat Thursday in Costa Maya and went to look for you."

"*What?*" I ask. "He went to look for me? What was he thinking?"

"He wasn't. Neither of us was. We were such a mess, Mae. You have no idea what it was like. No one would help us, and he just got tired of waiting." She looks me up and down. "Are you...okay?"

"I'm fine," I promise her. "I mean, tired and hungry, but I'm okay. I'll explain everything, but first, we have to find him. Did he say where he was going?"

"Um, some island called... I can't remember the name..."

"Isla de los Robados?" I ask, recalling the name Danny had given me.

"Yes! That's it! Is that where you were? Was he right?"

"Yes, but only briefly." I wave away the terrified look on her face. "I'm okay, I promise. Right now, my only concern is finding him. He wasn't on the island when I was there. At least I didn't see him. Is there anything else he told you? We need to go to the police."

"Yeah, of course. That was all he said. I was trying to go with him, but he left me. He said I needed to be here to tell your parents what happened, in case he didn't make it back. *Which he will,*" she adds quickly, pulling me in for another hug. "Oh my gosh, I just can't believe you're here."

I'm not listening, still distracted by everything that's gone wrong. Even when I manage to get free, even when I find a way home, I'm still not with Blake. If he dies going after me, if we never see each other again when I am so close to having him back, I'm not sure what I'll do. I'm not sure how I'll survive.

"Hey..." Florence whispers, rubbing my back. "It's okay. We'll find him."

This is all my dad's fault. The realization slams into my chest. If I lose Blake, it will be my dad's fault. And Blake will be gone because he met me. Because he loved me. It's all too much.

"Have you talked to my parents?"

"Yeah, they should be here any day. They're driving in." Her eyes widen. "Oh, my gosh! I just realized... They're going to be so happy you're here. They've been so worried. We should call them." She unlocks her phone, scrolling through her call log.

"No," I say too quickly. "No. Florence, you can't let them know I'm here. Don't tell them you found me. Let them think I'm still missing."

"Wait, what?" She looks up at me with furrowed brows. "Are you joking? Why?"

I drop my chin to my chest, the words burning me from the inside even before I say them. "My dad is... He's the reason I was taken. He did this."

She laughs as if it's a terrible joke. "What? *No.*" She shakes her head. "Why would you say that?"

"Because it's true. Look, we need to go to the police station. I'll explain everything there."

"Let's go then." She doesn't understand, and I couldn't expect her to, but she asks no further questions. Instead, she takes my hand, lifts her bags, and leads me to her rental car. She's everything I could possibly need to get through this.

We stop next to the trunk when I spy two officers standing next to a squad car, studying everyone who leaves the port.

"Excuse me! Officers!" I take a step toward them, a hand in the air. "Can you help us?"

"Is everything alright?" the first officer asks, her hand moving to her gun in its holster. My throat goes dry.

"No. My husband is missing. He was supposed to be on the boat, but he got off, and now we don't know where he is."

"Ma'am, slow down," the second officer says, his voice steady and calm. He holds his hands out as if to say I shouldn't be dramatic. If he only knew what I've been through... "What's your husband's name?"

"Blake Barlowe."

The officers exchange a glance.

"What is it?" I demand, my knees weak. What do they know? Have they already found him? Did he make it back? Has something happened?

The female officer's eyes take in the full sight of me, head to toe. She sucks in a breath, preparing to say something, but the male officer speaks over her.

"Your husband's name is Blake Barlowe?"

"Yes."

"And he was on board this cruise ship?"

"Yes."

He looks at his partner again. "And he's missing?"

"Yes," I say, trying to hide my exasperation.

"Funny..." he says softly.

"What's funny?" Florence asks.

"We're here waiting to meet a Blake Barlowe... Because his wife"—his brows shoot up when he looks at me pointedly—"is supposed to be missing."

Later, at the police station, I tell them everything. I tell them about the bartender, Benny, drugging me. How he must've drugged my water at the bar that night and how he chased me to the elevator before I blacked out. How I woke up on the second ship. I tell them how the men treated me, what Danny told me about what happened to him, and where his ship was. I tell them about my father. I tell them how, at the end of the day, this all leads back to him.

Florence sits beside me, listening in silence as I

recount every brutal minute over the last few days. She cries and holds my hand, assuring me she's here and that she'll be here.

Then, when it's all over, when there's nothing left to tell, I wait. We leave the police station with a warning to stay in the area—not that I'd planned to go anywhere without Blake—and return to the beach.

I tell myself I've done everything I can.

Everything to fix my karma.

I just need the universe to send my husband home to me.

Florence and I sit on the beach. If she's hungry or tired, she doesn't mention it. We sit, arms linked together over our knees, and we watch the horizon. Several hours pass, each one more difficult than the last.

If I were a braver woman, perhaps I would rent a boat myself and go after him. It's what he would've done— what he *did* do. The longer I sit, the more the guilt eats at me.

My last act as his wife was to meet another man for drinks, and he still braved the entire ocean for me. I don't deserve him.

Maybe this is karma, after all.

When a police officer walks up to us as the sun is setting, something in his expression turns my gut to stone. He drops down on the sand next to us.

"Evening, Mrs. Barlowe."

"Did you find him?" I beg him to say yes. To tell me he's fine. That he's coming back to me right now.

"Ma'am, they..." He swallows and looks out over the

water. "I'm so sorry to be the one to tell you this. When our officers were on the way to the island you talked about, they found a boat. We believe it's the one he'd stolen."

Stolen. I hate the way he says the word, like Blake's a criminal.

"What does that mean?" Florence asks, holding my hand tighter. "You found a boat. Was he on it? Did you find him?"

"No, ma'am. I'm sorry. Based on where they found it, there's a good chance he traveled straight through the path of a storm last night. It looks like... Well, we're afraid he may have fallen victim to it."

"Fallen victim? You mean he died? He drowned?" It's all too reminiscent of Danny. I can't do this again. I can't know that he died while trying to save me. I can't live without him. Brutal sobs rip through me when the officer nods. "No! *No!* He can't die. You have to look for him. Did you go to the island? Did you search everywhere? He can't just be gone!" I fight against what he's saying with every ounce of strength I have. I can't breathe. My chest is too tight. There's no oxygen left on this beach.

I can't lose him.
I can't lose him.
I can't lose him.

"They're still going to search the island. Of course. Right now, our priority has changed. A new team will head out for the island, but our primary team is searching the water for any sign of your husband." I must give some indication that his words have given me hope because he quickly adds, "There's very little chance we'll find him at this stage. With tide changes and the depth we're dealing with..." He stops himself, his kind eyes dancing between mine. He wants me to understand what he's saying, but I don't. I can't. It's impossible. "The boat's completely trashed and there was no one on board, ma'am. I'm so sorry. As I said, we have a team searching the water now. They'll do what they can, but...you should start preparing yourself for the worst. If there's anyone you'd like to call, now would be the time. I'm sorry," he repeats, already resigning Blake to a watery grave. "I wish I had better news."

When he stands and walks away, I collapse in the sand. Florence falls with me, holding me, squeezing me as if I might fall apart if she doesn't hold me tightly enough.

This can't be happening. He can't be gone.

He can't.

I can't lose him.

Not like this.

"We have to go." I turn to face her, pulling out of her grasp. "We have to go now. We have to rent a boat. We have to find him."

She's quiet, watching me. She doesn't immediately argue, but when I stand, she remains seated. "Go where, Mae? Where will we go?"

"Out there!" I wave my arms in the general direction of the ocean. "To the island. To wherever they found his boat."

"Neither of us knows anything about driving a boat,

nor do we know where the island is. Or his boat, for that matter." She shakes her head softly. "He wouldn't want this for you. He was out there to save you and he—"

"And look what that did to him! Look what I did to him, Flo!" I shout, angry at her, angry at myself, angry at Blake for ever getting on that stupid boat, for not just letting me go. He didn't deserve this.

"You didn't do this." Now she's on her feet. She grips both my shoulders. "Mae, look at me. This isn't your fault. We don't know anything yet. They could still find him."

"So what, I'm just supposed to sit here? Do nothing? Call his parents and say they should come in case..." I choke on my words, unable to finish the sentence. "I can't lose him, Flo. I can't. I won't survive it."

"I know," she whispers, her eyes tired.

"I could call Danny," I tell her, searching for an answer as if it's water in a barren desert. "I could call my dad and make him give me Danny's number. Danny's crew could search for him."

"Does your dad have Danny's number? He doesn't know he's alive."

"He would have a way to contact someone," I insist.

"But would he give it to you? The police told you not to contact him. That we're supposed to let him arrive here thinking you're still missing."

"I don't care what the police said! I just want my husband back!" I shout.

"I know." She squeezes my shoulders, her voice gentle. She's like a parent trying to convince me to take my medicine. A kindergarten teacher trying to coax me into her classroom on the first day of school. "I know you do. But...would he even give it to you? If he knows you're alive and you're asking for a way to contact the traffickers, even if you don't tell him it's Danny, would he have any reason to help you? All you'd be doing is tipping him off and putting more people at risk."

"I don't care about anyone else," I sob. "I just want him." With that, I collapse into her arms finally, and she wraps me up, rubbing my back with both hands as if I haven't just said the most cruel, selfish thing I could say.

"It's going to be okay," she promises. "We aren't giving up."

Even as she says it, I can sense the defeat in her tone. She's giving up on him.

I can't give up on him.

I can't do any of this without him. I don't want to.

"He can't be gone," I whisper. My throat is tight, my skin too hot. I can't think. My body feels like it might explode with grief. Perhaps it would be better that way. Better to have physical pain than this.

Against her skin, I suck in a ragged breath. *It wasn't enough.*

I did everything I could to make things right, to be a good person, to fix this, to come home to him, and none of it mattered. At the end of the day, the ocean did what it does best and stole him from me.

No matter how hard I tried, I lost him anyway.

CHAPTER TWENTY-NINE

MAE

The next few hours pass in a blur.

Florence stays with me, leaving only to replenish our supply of water and sunscreen. At one point, she offers to get us a hotel room, but I don't want to leave this spot. I can't.

As the night drags on, Zach arrives to offer me comfort. There's an apology in his eyes that makes me sick. We did this. If I'd never met with him that night, maybe this wouldn't have happened. If I'd stayed in my room with Blake, maybe I would still be safe. Maybe Blake would be alive. I realize then no matter what happens, I don't want him. I only want Blake. I was so blind not to see that before.

I'll never be able to look at Zach and see anything other than the man who was with me the night I betrayed Blake.

The last man I kissed before my husband died.

I hate myself.

I hate him.

I find myself falling in and out of sleep on the sand, starting to refuse drinks and food. How can I eat when Blake is dead? How can I just move on? It would've been easier if they'd left me on the boat. If I'd gone with Danny. If he'd never set me free.

I squeeze my eyes shut, rolling so my face is in the sand. I have no tears left. I feel dry and bitter and broken, as if, given enough time, I could wither away, turn into sand myself, and blow away.

At least then, we'd be together.

When I hear Florence say my name, I hardly register it. It isn't until she's up on her feet, pulling me to mine, that I realize something's happening.

"Mae, look! Mae, look there!" she shouts, pointing at a police boat that has neared the shore.

Did they find him? Are they going to tell me this is over? Confirm what I already know?

I focus on the boat, on my breathing.

I can do this. Blake needs me to do this.

"Is that..." Florence goes quiet. She looks down at me just as I realize what she's seeing. There's someone in the boat with the officers.

I hold my breath, praying. Begging the universe for the biggest mercy.

Please.

Please.

Please.

My vision blurs as the officers step from the boat,

reaching forward to help the man with the life jacket up from where he's sitting. My throat goes dry.

I can't breathe.

Can't think.

When he comes into view, my knees go weak. Florence, sensing it, keeps a firm hold on my arms. Beside me, she's openly sobbing. There's no mistaking Blake as he gets out. One of the officers points in our direction, and Blake's head turns toward me. When we lock eyes, the air deflates from my lungs. He collapses onto the sand on his knees.

The officers gather around him, helping him to lie flat. I run, taking off at full speed until I reach him. I drop to the sand, running a hand over his chest, taking his hand in mine.

"I can't believe it's you..." he whispers.

"Me either," I say, through sobs of my own. "I thought I lost you." I kiss his fingers.

"What happened?" Florence asks the officers. "Where did you find him?"

"We found him floating a few miles from where we discovered his boat. He had the sense to wear a life jacket and, at some point, he found some driftwood to hold on to. It's a miracle, frankly," one of the officers says, grinning at me.

"Are you real?" Blake whispers, holding my face with one hand.

"I'm real," I cry. "And you're real. This is real."

"I won't...believe it"—he struggles to sit up—"till I get

a kiss." The officers chuckle, looking away as I lean forward and press my lips to his.

"I love you so much." His warm, salty scent fills my nose, and I never want to let him go again.

His eyes close as he leans back onto the sand again, and a single tear streams down his cheek. "Very, very real."

He's home.

We're together.

He holds my hand as two paramedics appear and begin looking him over. I can't let go, and they don't ask me to. If it's up to me, I'll never let go of his hand again.

Somehow, we made it through this. Against all the odds, he came back to me, just like I came back to him.

That's all that matters to me. The rest is background noise. As long as we're together, everything else will be okay.

CHAPTER THIRTY

MARTHA LEIGHTON

THREE YEARS LATER

"Are you ready, Mom?" Mae asks as we walk into the tiny room in the prison where my son awaits. My heart thuds in my chest. It's the first time I'll see him outside of a courtroom since he was eight years old.

He's grown into such a man.

I never thought I'd see him again. Certainly not under these circumstances.

I can't believe he's still alive.

When he comes into view, no amount of preparation could've ever made me ready for this.

"Mom." He stands from behind the table they've seated him at. He's in prison but is allowed certain privileges for helping the FBI bring down the trafficking ring he once ran. My husband, also in prison, did not receive such privileges, nor should he have.

"My baby," I cry. It's the only phrase I can muster. I reach for him, but the guard at the door stops me.

"No touching."

"I'm sorry! I'm so sorry!" I say quickly. Why is it easier to apologize to this stranger than it is my own flesh and blood? "You look so grown up," I whisper as we sit.

"So do you," he says.

"Your hair..." I touch my own hair. "It got darker. It looks nice."

When he smiles, I spot the evidence of the life he's lived. A scar near his mouth, a once-broken nose. My beautiful boy is nearly unrecognizable, but of course, I do recognize him. How could I not? He looks just like his father.

"I'm probably a lot skinnier than the last time you saw me. Less hair," I joke.

"Every bit as beautiful." His smile remains untouched. It is as perfect as I remember, with a few extra teeth.

"I'm so sorry, Danny," I manage to choke out. "If I'd known... He never... I never thought or suspected..."

"I know," he says, cutting me off. "Mom, you don't have to do this. You don't owe me an apology. I know you didn't know. I know it's not your fault."

"It is though," I whine, clasping my trembling hands together on the table. "You did this because of me. It was all because of me."

"It wasn't. It wasn't your plan. Dad did this. Not you."

I nod. It's not nearly as simple as that, and we both know it. "I loved you, Danny. You were my... You were my baby boy. I never stopped loving you. Never stopped hoping we'd find you. We came back here every year, and I'd walk along the ocean and talk to you. If I'd known..." I look down, drying my tears. "I'm just so sorry."

"I know. I knew I was loved. I knew you loved me. It's why I did it. I wanted to protect you. You're my mom. And I don't regret it, for the record, if it meant saving you." His face is solemn. Serious. "I'd do it a hundred times over."

I can't bring myself to respond. I look down, moving my hands to my lap. Next to me, Mae reaches over and rubs my arm. "We'll visit every chance we get," she tells her brother. "I'm sorry we couldn't come until today. They wouldn't let us."

"I'm just glad you're here now," Danny says.

"So, you don't hate me?" she asks gently. For turning him in, she means. Telling the police who he was and where to find him. Without her, he'd still be free.

"I told you to do what you had to do, and you did," he answers.

"Is there anything we can bring you?" I ask him. "Maybe some snacks? I don't know what they'll let you have here."

His smile is patronizing as he releases a breath through his nose. I realize I'm talking about prison as if it were summer camp. "I'm fine, Mom. I can take care of myself."

"You always have been able to," I whisper, my voice breaking. "But you shouldn't have to."

"Enough about me," he says. "How have you been? How's the treatment going?"

We talk for a while longer, though I'm not quite sure how to catch up on the last twenty-six years in the half hour they give us to visit. When the guard warns us our time is up, we promise to come back next week.

"Take care of yourself, big brother," Mae says as we stand. "We love you."

I blow a kiss his way, watching as the guard replaces his handcuffs and leads him out of the room.

When we're alone, Mae rubs a hand on my back. "You okay?"

Always checking on me...

My daughter is a good one. A firm believer in karma and being a perfect person. It's why she turned my son and husband in. Why she's constantly cooking dinner for Florence and whatever guy she's dating this week. Why she moved me in with her and Blake, so she can take care of me around the clock.

She believes when you do bad things, the universe will punish you like it has my husband. And when you do good things, like telling the truth, it will reward you, like it did when it sent Blake back to her.

I study the two of them in front of me, hand in hand, happy as clams.

I, on the other hand, am more skeptical.

I never did anything bad before I got sick. I was a good mother. A loving wife. I took care of my kids, my house. I went back to the store to pay for groceries when I realized the cashier had missed something. I taught my kids manners, had them water the garden for our elderly neighbor when she had the flu for a full week in the summer. I was a good person. I'd firmly tipped whatever karmic scales may exist in my favor.

But, in the end, the universe didn't care. I got sick. I almost died. I've fought for my life for the better half of the last nearly three decades.

Good person or not, it punished me anyway.

But now, even after all the terrible things I've done, even after convincing Bill my plan was the only way, that it had to be done or I would die, I'm still here. When you compare the two of us, you might say he was the better person. He convinced me to save Mae back then, not to let them take her, too. I would've let them. I was that desperate, and we could've gotten more for her.

He called her our *rainy day fund* in case things got bad in the future. He did the right thing—the good thing, the noble thing—and saved her life when I thought it was too risky. And look where that got him. Look where nobility landed him.

In fact, by the end of it, after everything I did, I still got both of my kids back, plus the money and the treatments, and somehow I managed to escape any of the blame.

Karma or no karma, I'm the winner here.

I'm still alive.

I want to live, you see. More than anything else in this world, I want to keep living. And *that's* what I believe in. More than being a good person. More than doing the right thing. More than karma. More than family. More than love.

Sheer determination above all else.

It's never let me down.

WOULD YOU RECOMMEND YOU CAN TRUST ME?

If you enjoyed this story, please consider leaving me a quick review. It doesn't have to be long—just a few words will do. Who knows? Your review might be the thing that encourages a future reader to take a chance on my work!
To leave a review, please visit:
https://mybook.to/youcantrustme

Let everyone know how much you loved
You Can Trust Me on Goodreads:
https://bit.ly/youcantrustmebook

STAY UP TO DATE ON EVERYTHING KMOD!

Thank you so much for reading this story. I'd love to invite you to sign up for my mailing list and text alerts so we can be sure you don't miss my next release.

Sign up for my mailing list here:
kierstenmodglinauthor.com/nlsignup

Sign up for my text alerts here:
kierstenmodglinauthor.com/textalerts

ACKNOWLEDGMENTS

As always, I should start by thanking my amazing husband and sweet little girl—thank you for doing life with me and for making it fun. I love you both so much and am incredibly grateful to get to celebrate every success with you! Thank you for being my cheerleaders, my sounding boards, and for coming along for every ride.

To my wonderful editor, Sarah West—thank you for seeing every story through the rubble and helping me turn it into something I'm proud of. I'm so thankful for your insights, advice, and knowledge.

To the awesome proofreading team at My Brother's Editor—thank you for making my stories shine! I'm so grateful to work with you!

To my loyal readers (AKA the #KMod Squad)—thank you for asking for this story! I had no idea how badly I wanted to tell it until the requests started coming in and, as always, I'm so thankful for your support with this and everything else. Thank you for being such a dream come true, for cheering me on, for being so enthusiastic over every book, and for loving my characters and wild ideas as much as I do! I hope this cruise thriller was everything you hoped for!

To my book club/gang/besties—Sara, both Erins,

June, Heather, and Dee—thank you for being my weekly dose of laughter and good times. I love you girls and couldn't do this without you!

To my bestie, Emerald O'Brien—thank you for being my best friend, for celebrating every success and helping me through every failure, for being the one I go to when I have a new idea and the one I go to when I'm out of ideas. I'm so grateful to share the moon with you, friend. Love you.

To Becca and Lexy—thank you for all you do for me!

Last but certainly not least, to you, dear reader—thank you for taking a chance on this story and supporting my art. Just by being here, you've made a dream come true for me. When I write my stories, I'm thinking of you. Wondering which parts will shock you, which characters you'll love, hate, or be suspicious of, and hoping that you'll enjoy it as much as I enjoyed writing it. Whether this was your first Kiersten Modglin book or your 39th, I hope it was everything you hoped for and nothing like you expected.

ABOUT THE AUTHOR

KIERSTEN MODGLIN is an Amazon Top 10 bestselling author of psychological thrillers. Her books have sold over a million copies and been translated into multiple languages. Kiersten is a member of International Thriller Writers, Novelists, Inc., and the Alliance of Independent Authors. She is a KDP Select All-Star and a recipient of *ThrillerFix's* Best Psychological Thriller Award, *Suspense Magazine's* Best Book of 2021 Award, a 2022 Silver Falchion for Best Suspense, and a 2022 Silver Falchion for Best Overall Book of 2021. Kiersten grew up in rural western Kentucky and later relocated to Nashville, Tennessee, where she now lives with her family. Kiersten's readers across the world lovingly refer to her as "KMod." A binge-watching expert, psychology fanatic, and *indoor* enthusiast, Kiersten enjoys rainy days spent with her favorite people and evenings with her nose in a book.

Sign up for Kiersten's newsletter here:
kierstenmodglinauthor.com/nlsignup

Sign up for text alerts from Kiersten here:
kierstenmodglinauthor.com/textalerts

kierstenmodglinauthor.com
www.facebook.com/kierstenmodglinauthor
www.facebook.com/groups/kmodsquad
www.twitter.com/kmodglinauthor
www.instagram.com/kierstenmodglinauthor
www.tiktok.com/@kierstenmodglinauthor
www.goodreads.com/kierstenmodglinauthor
www.bookbub.com/authors/kiersten-modglin
www.amazon.com/author/kierstenmodglin

ALSO BY KIERSTEN MODGLIN

Widow Falls

Missing Daughter

The Reunion

Tell Me the Truth

The Dinner Guests

If You're Reading This...

A Quiet Retreat

The Family Secret

Don't Go Down There

Wait for Dark

ARRANGEMENT TRILOGY

The Arrangement (Book 1)

The Amendment (Book 2)

The Atonement (Book 3)

THE MESSES SERIES

The Cleaner (Book 1)

The Healer (Book 2)

The Liar (Book 3)

The Prisoner (Book 4)

NOVELLAS

The Long Route: A Lover's Landing Novella

The Stranger in the Woods: A Crimson Falls Novella

Made in United States
North Haven, CT
12 July 2023

38872362R00168